"Elegantly written and deceptively humorous, Dolki Min's bombastic debut novel, *Walking Practice*, is a haunting examination of survival, gender, and the complexity of the human experience. A tremendous literary achievement."

—Eric LaRocca, author of *Things Have Gotten Worse Since We Last Spoke and Other Misfortunes*

"*Walking Practice* is an unforgettable survival story of an alien trying to survive as a human on a hostile planet. This unique and imaginative, weird and delicate sci-fi is a considerate exploration of our social structures: the gender conventions, queerness, and discrimination against the weak. A radical, darkly funny, spine-tingling story, perfect for fans of Matt Haig's *The Humans* and Michel Faber's *Under the Skin*."

—J. M. Lee, bestselling author of *Broken Summer*

"Surreal, compelling, and utterly unique."

—*BuzzFeed*

"*Walking Practice* explores the burden of gender expectations, the struggle of having a flesh prison body, having to feed yourself and wanting to be loved, and even the awkwardness of dealing with other people on the subway. But what really makes this story sing is the uniqueness of the narrator's voice—both compelling and witty. . . . It is moving and funny, critical and crass. This one is for anyone who is made to feel like an alien in their own body."

—Tor.com

"Through this weird, funny, deeply earnest book about a killer alien who doesn't fit in on Earth, Min has crafted a queer novel about feeling out of place in one's body and its surroundings. . . . The evident pleasure with which Min has drawn this character makes for a vibrant and memorable fictional encounter with an otherness that's not, in the end, so different."

—*New York Times Book Review*

"An alien arrives on Earth, hungry for love. The narrator of Min's dark satire . . . is a shape-shifting alien who crash-landed here 15 years ago. In that time, it's sampled all sorts of sustenance on our planet, but only human flesh truly satisfies. So it uses dating apps (username: Hunting4luv) to quell its cravings for sex and sustenance. . . . Entertaining and surprising . . . A slim, sui generis allegory on romance and its discontents."

—*Kirkus Reviews* (starred review)

"Who would come up with a story about a shapeshifting alien who crashlands on Earth, learns to walk by hunting humans, and then is forced to confront their sins of survival while critiquing humankind's marginalization of

Others? Dolki Min, that's who. And who would read such a story? You, if you know what's good for you."

—Ms. magazine

"There's bleak comedy aplenty in Dolki Min's *Walking Practice*—which makes sense, given that protagonist Mumu is a shapeshifting alien who chats with unwitting guys on the internet and then devours them. But this isn't simply an exercise in the overlap of horror and humor; instead, Mumu's observations on human gender roles and the fraught nature of nearly every interaction in the narrative give this book a substantial narrative weight, even as the text and translation also factor in some play-fulness."

—Words Without Borders

"On the surface, this smart debut novel (translated from the Korean by Victoria Caudle) is a fun story about an alien who finds men on dating apps and eats them to stay alive. But underneath lies a potent critique of gender norms and an exploration of what it feels like to not fit in your body or your surroundings."

—*New York Times* "Books We Recommend"

WALKING PRACTICE

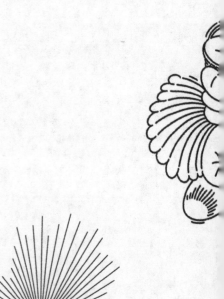

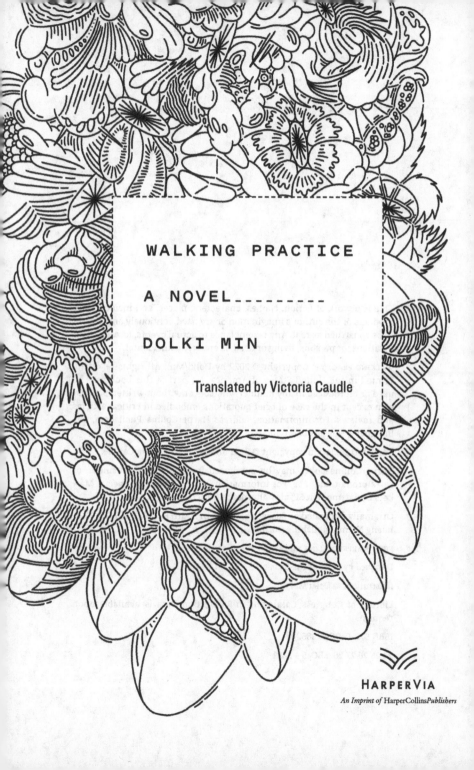

WALKING PRACTICE

A NOVEL _____

DOLKI MIN

Translated by Victoria Caudle

HarperVia

An Imprint of HarperCollins*Publishers*

HarperCollins books may be purchased for educational, business, or sales promotional use. For information, please email the Special Markets Department at SPsales@harpercollins.com.

Originally published as *Bohaeng Yeonseup* in South Korea in 2022 by Eunhaeng Namu Publishing Co., Ltd.

FIRST HARPERCOLLINS PAPERBACK PUBLISHED IN 2024

Designed by Janet Evans-Scanlon

Illustrations © Dolki Min

Library of Congress Cataloging-in-Publication Data is available upon request.

ISBN 978-0-06-325862-4

24 25 26 27 28 LBC 5 4 3 2 1

WALKING PRACTICE

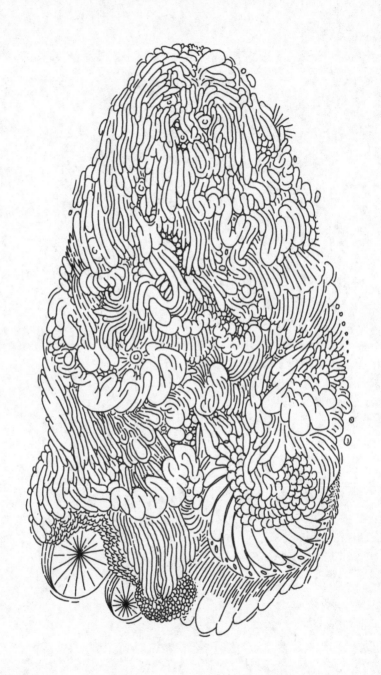

'm off to work early. This isn't a regular occurrence. It's out of necessity today because he says his house is only empty in the morning. He has too many choice qualities for me to let him slip through my fingers. And by "qualities," I of course mean physical ones. I don't know what kind of human he is: what he likes to eat, his favorite color, the kind of music he's into these days. None of these interest me. We've simply exchanged a few words in a chat room and made a date. A fairly good-looking twenty-seven-year-old male—height 173 cm, weight 65 kg. And an eight-inch cock. That's all I know. Oh, and one more thing, he lives at the top of a sixteen-story apartment building.

Right now, I'm heading there on the subway. You have no idea how relieved I am to be here, sitting pretty. So overjoyed, I could burst into tears. No matter how you couch it, riding the subway feels disgusting: you dangle like ripe fruit from a hanging vine, squeezed in among humans swarming like bees. Especially on a day like this, when I'm not in top form, it gets harder to find my center of gravity on only two legs. That being said, the subway is so much better than the bus. It's a miracle if I don't fall over in those rattling steel-barred cells they call buses.

It must have been two or three years after I settled down here. I didn't really have anything to do, nor any place in particular I needed to be, so I prowled the streets until, exhausted, with nothing to show for it, I dragged my body to a bus stop. No, I must have brought myself there unconsciously. I didn't plan to take the bus home. But in those days, I was unaware that the subway stopped running at a certain time. I had seen people hail taxis a few times, but the prospect of trying it myself overwhelmed me with fear. Back then, just raising a hand up so that a driver could see it was an onerous task. I wouldn't have been able to endure the scrutiny of someone looking directly at the shape of my hand. Just imagining it made my hair stand on end. If I am to be completely honest, it keeps me from catching taxis to this day. Once, I plucked up the courage and stuck my hand out to hail one and a toe popped out on my elbow; the taxi driver, eyes nearly popping out of his head, yanked the wheel and sped away. From then on, I've always kept my distance from taxis.

But there are steep stairs on buses. There are no-step buses now, but they've only just been introduced to the fleet. The first time I took public transportation, the height of the stairs was much greater than I expected, and I worried if I would even be able to climb them. All the stairs I had practiced on until then had been of negligible height and width. I grappled with gravity and climbed aboard the bus, claiming a small victory. The ascent was so laborious that I felt my bones might crumble, but the sense of accomplishment pleased me greatly. I thought the only thing left was to deposit my fare and find a seat. But before I could even catch my breath, the bus driver stomped on the accelerator, and I tumbled to the back and got wedged under the bench. I was coated in dirt and sweat and droplets of blood. Shocked, I couldn't move a muscle. Nor did I have the leisure to feel shame. The driver swore like nothing I'd heard before, and the other passengers jeered. They didn't even try to help. It never crossed their minds to reach out a hand, grab me by the tentacle, and pull me up. Ah, I was in far too disgusting of a state to arouse sympathy and a willingness to help. The high degree of concentration required to maintain my humanlike form was in tatters; my eyeballs drifted in opposite directions; my arms and legs contorted; and my abdomen swelled up like a balloon. They must have been thinking, if only you were just a little less repulsive, I would step forward and lend a hand. I don't remember how I managed to get home after that. It was as if someone had extracted the splinters of memory from inside my head like you would pluck a thorn from your skin. When I opened my eyes, I was sprawled out on the floor of my inky black living room. My shoes and clothes had burst apart like the carcass of a cat crushed beneath the tire of a car, unable to withstand my form. Painfully hungry, I could have killed on the spot.

I am hungry now. In fact, I only brave the humidity and the piss-stink of this environment because it is all worth it to get to him. Squeezing tight, I hug the bulky backpack balanced on my thighs. Inside it, all of my bright and shiny tools are sweetly tucked away in perfect order. They will help me satisfy my hunger. Whenever the subway rumbles, I keep my ear trained on the clinking and clanking sounds coming from inside my bag. I forget my hunger for the moment and fully relax. Drowsiness wells up within me, like it does when you sit in stillness and listen to the drip, drip, dropping of rain falling outside your window. The stress brought on by the train car being packed with passengers slowly fades away, and I drift into a shallow sleep.

I wake up when my bag falls onto the floor with a dull *koong*. People turn their heads, eyes darting about, searching for the source of the noise. And once they see it is no big deal, they once again focus on their own business. While I wrestle the bag back into position on the tops of my thighs, a variable I hadn't considered comes to mind.

You. You, dear reader, must be curious about my gender. Perhaps you are even feeling a little anxious. Or you might have scraped together clues from what I've said and how I've said it, constructing my gender to your own design. Regardless as to whether you are right or wrong, you will have come to your own conclusions.

After I was thrown to this place against my wishes, I did my best to survive; I discovered that there are many of you who, when meeting someone new, first take their gender into account. I also get the impression that it is only after a gender has been assigned that you are seen as human. This process is completed so naturally, and with such alacrity, that you aren't even aware of automatically assigning gender to others. But there is a time when you do become aware: when you are uncertain of another's gender. You grow anxious when, wherever you may be, you encounter someone who you cannot immediately classify as male or female—or, to put it another way, when the "evidence" for your gender judgment is conflicted. This is because, according to your narrow system of understanding, it is difficult to decide how to interact—for example, what honorific should you use—with someone whose body you simply cannot decipher.

You, dear reader, are an old hand at the gender-matching game. No doubt about it! From a tender age you have guessed the gender of countless humans whose bodies are covered by clothes, coming to conclusions based on the gender you believe corresponds to the shape of genitals you believe match up with the remaining exposed parts of their bodies, and you have lived your lives in certainty, believing the result of your deductions to be true. The problem is, however, that you do not acknowledge the mistakes you have made and will continue to make. No one knows that the game itself is a mistake.

Oh, I do apologize. I have yet to reveal my gender, leaving you, my dear reader, trembling with anxiety. How cruel! Well then, I will alleviate your anxiety. I'll now give you succor. Shall I put you at ease? Hahaha, shall I ease your mind? I will relieve you. I am

female.

That is, at least I am until I have completed my journey to that man's house and taken care of my work. What does it mean to be a woman? Among other things, it means that you have to decorate yourself and act like a woman. No one has ordered me to do so; I willingly take on the responsibility. For if the performance is not carried out properly, I am nothing more than a monstrosity. It is imperative that I am not seen as a monster. My work and my life depend on it. Are you listening? Pay close attention to what I have to say. This is purely a matter of survival. If I don't become a woman—or, when the occasion calls for it, a man—I will starve to death. If I mean to satisfy my hunger, then scarcely living will not suffice. We must always do more. Whether it is keeping two feet balanced on the bus or subway, or becoming a woman . . .

Ah, now it's almost time to get off the train. There are so0O0o many people on the subway. Sometimes it feels excruciatingly crowded. All of these people who poke their heads out and start swarming as soon as the sun rises, where do they hide themselves away at night? If for just one day they put an end to their ceaselessly stepping feet and constantly wagging tongues, I bet they'd all seize up in shock!

I'm worried that not enough people will get off the train at the next stop. The mere thought paralyzes me. Even more so when I'm sitting far away from the automatic doors. I lack the confidence to bore through the mass of tightly packed people, standing close as trees in a rarely traveled forest. And I can't bear the thought of having to spit out, "Excuse me, please! I'm getting off!" Whenever startled or nervous, my voice cracks like a crowing rooster. It becomes something utterly unhuman. Even if I focus on vibrating my vocal cords and shaping my lips to produce an approximately human voice, if people ignore me or don't get out of my way, I'll be hopelessly trapped.

And then I won't be able to meet him in time, and even if he kindly overlooks my lateness, it will still fuck up the timing of my next appointment. My plans for the whole day could be a bust. Oh, I am so frightened now. I do apologize. There's no reason for you to sit here listening to me fret. But I would be ever so pleased if you stick it out till the very end. I am a being wholly unrelated to you, but I am not living on some frozen planet six million light-years away. I am right beside you.

The screen doors slide open. The passengers are hurriedly fucking off like blood that finally penetrated an artery that's been blocked for ten years. Who knows, I could even ardently love one of them. I quickly pack away my useless delusions and, feeling a bit dizzy, pass through the open doors. Once, about nine years ago, I had my side rudely chomped down on by the subway doors. The doors have never apologized, and I still have not forgiven them. That's why I am chronically light-headed and will continue to be so. But it doesn't matter. As long as I manage to alight without incident, does a bit of dizziness matter? Nope. There is no problem there. The real problem is

the nearly 140 steps

of the stairs. The stairs that I must tackle in order to transfer trains stare back at me murderously. There is no elevator or escalator to rescue me. People racing down the steps unintentionally force me down deeper into this hellhole. Ordinarily, I'd hyperventilate, and the bottoms of my feet would ulcerate, but I somehow manage to make my way down with comparative ease. However, today's sky is the type of overcast that can snap to thunder, lightning, and heavy showers in a flash. For me, this type of weather is lethal. Your gravity weighs down on me sixfold. That isn't to say there are no ways to combat it. Within the straight stream of people, I cut a cautious diagonal, inch by inch making my way to the handrail and grab on. I don't know how many people's feet I step on or shoulders I collide with, but it doesn't matter. What matters most is my life. If a weakling like me pushes against them as I pass, all that will happen is that they'll be thrown off balance briefly and foul language will slip out, but the chance of them tumbling down the stairs and cracking open their skull is minimal. I do not wish to crack open my head. I've fallen down flights of stairs countless times and haven't cracked it open yet, but I have not even a hair's width inclination to leave the life-or-death of my head to fortune. In case you've forgotten, I'll mention it again—I have an enormous hiking bag strapped to my back. It weighs about 10 kg. It is nothing short of miraculous that I haven't been flattened like fish jerky and have doggedly persisted for so long. Would a suitcase be better? I have no idea. But, dear reader, thanks to your sincere support and the sturdy handrail, I manage to step onto the slick, slippery floor without incident. However, I do need to take the time to salvage and separate my toes, which have melted into one stumpy block. I lean into a nook in the wall, peel off my sock, pry my precious toes apart, and wiggle them. I take several deep breaths to compose myself before standing up to catch the next train.

I am in an elevator with the old humans rising up to the surface of the Earth. The sound of the rain grows closer. It's impatient to maul the people below it. But I am not foolish enough to be beaten by the rain. I unfurl my umbrella as the sweltering air pierces my nose.

I check the map as I start to penetrate the atmosphere blocking my path, the air as thick as my body. It seems that even the air gets tired of pretending to be empty now and then. It feels like chipping away at a rock face with your skin. Every person holds an umbrella, splashing as they pass me. I, too, earnestly and clumsily pass them by. They pay even less attention to the people around them than when the weather is clear. Maybe it's because they all want to get home quickly? They mostly keep their eyes pointed straight ahead. Please continue to be so inattentive. Please only give me attention when I want it.

The gloomy, rain-drenched building grows farther away. A gleaming car cuts through a stream of black water

making the road slippery. The intermittent traffic lights restrain the cars every so often, but fourteen years ago, those guys couldn't hold me back. In complete ignorance, I tried crossing the road at a red light and was mercilessly run over by a sweet little car. From that day on I became incapable of crossing. Thanks to this, the possibility of my crossing over into the afterlife by way of a traffic accident is greatly reduced, haha.

I get a text.

—Where are you?

Clasping my umbrella in one shivering hand, I send a quick reply.

—Almost there.
—You sure you'll be able to find it?
—I'm sure.
—Don't ring the doorbell, knock.
—Got it.

I arrive at the apartment block. The buildings are a deep blue-green color, as if covered in moss or lichen. It isn't hard to find building 210. Since the buildings are fairly old, paint is peeling off in some spots, but the black lettering is crisp and clear. Even I, with my poor eyesight, had no problem at all making them out. As soon as I discovered the lettering that marked the building as 210, my heart began to pound wildly. I never get used to it. Each time feels as new as the first and causes me to break out in a cold sweat. However, the amount of my nervousness is always repaid with the enormity of the pleasure I receive when my work is completed. Every day, I risk ruining my life through the smallest of mistakes as I go to meet strangers. That's why I must plan my work with meticulous precision. Even if something totally unexpected occurs, I have to be quick on my feet to handle it. I close my umbrella and shake off the wetness, and with confident steps I enter 210 and head straight to the elevator.

I go to press the button, but see red letters illuminated below the panel. The letters are so incredibly small and difficult to read that I have to bring my face so close my nose almost touches the wall, but I already know what the light under the numbers means. The elevator is down for maintenance, so either I have to buck up and take the stairs or wait until who knows when. I hastily flip through all the plans I had meticulously filed away in my mind, but I can't find any miraculous plan that could be used when faced with having to climb up sixteen flights of stairs. I tear at my innocent hair and in the end decide to text him for help. I couldn't tell you how many times, with trembling fingers, I typed out my message, erased it, and typed it again.

—Hey, did you know the elevator is down for maintenance?
—Oh really? I didn't know. Use the stairs.

I barely manage to contain my impulse to tear this human apart into little bitty pieces. Who said I didn't know there were stairs? But whenever an issue like this crops up, I must keep calm. Rash actions must be avoided. Discretion and more discretion. That is my long-serving credo. I can still vividly recall the tragedy that befell when I ignored it and acted as I pleased . . .

—Take your time, I'll be waiting.

Take my time? You'll be waiting? It's raining, I'm in a terrible mood, and this man is just begging to die. If perchance he chooses me as his mode of suicide, I will make him regret that decision down to the core of his marrow. The physical pain I will inflict will be so exquisite that he will lose himself in the sweet reality. As soon as he cries out for help, I will end him. I end my fantasy to focus on the task at hand. I don't know how to take his fucking joke of a response. He definitely won't come down to the first floor, but do you think, if I asked, he'd meet me on the eighth and give me a piggyback ride? It would even suffice if he'd get behind me and push. And if he won't do that, should I try asking if we could go to a nearby love hotel? That sounds reasonable.

But when I make the suggestion, this bastard lets my words bounce off the back of his ears. He makes it seem like if I don't want to climb up, I should just leave. So now I really must go up there. I've just got to burst into that room where he's lying on the bed shoving a finger up his nose and scratching his ass. For as much as he has viciously teased me, there is no way I'll let him wriggle out of my grasp. No fucking way!

Step by step I climb the sharp, chilly stairs, curling my fingers tightly around the handrail like the roots of a plant desperately searching for moisture. Regardless of my actions, the stairs wouldn't budge—if only they half-resembled an escalator!—and persist in their attack on me. These bastard stairs taunt me, *No matter what you do, you're gonna fall.* But not only do I have to put up with the hard-hearted staircase, but I have to wrestle with the sweat seeping out of my own pores. What started out like a slender, tickling stream, became like a river, then an ocean, soaking my whole body. My hair has pasted itself to the back of my neck and my cheeks and clearly has no intention of letting go. And what about the straps of my backpack, digging into my shoulders? It'll only hurt my mouth if I talk about how my knees and ankles feel like they are going to snap!

There's not even a booger's amount of support for me in this universe. My body is a filthy jerk that is constantly keeping its eyes peeled for any chance to betray me. I am certain of it. And I won't be fooled twice. Normally, it puts on a show of doing its all for me, of serving only me, but if given an inch, it'll give its owner a good bash to the head. There are a lot of times when this flesh suit is nothing more than cumbersome baggage that causes me pain. The sight of me trying to haul this body up the stairs is completely laughable.

This simply will not do. I have to take a little break. I flop down onto the landing and swallow the spit that was about to go down the wrong pipe. My heavy breathing settles, and I fish a glamorous two-liter water bottle out from my backpack. As if in the middle of stretching, I drop my chin and shove the bottle into my mouth. Not even a lifeform that never leaves the water could gulp it down as fast as I do. I put the bottle back into my bag and see another text pop up.

—What floor are you on?
—Six . . .
—Are you a sweaty person? I can't stand the smell. Well, I guess it doesn't matter since you can shower here. Take one as soon as you get here.
—Okay

If only I had known he was going to be this rude, I would not have begun to climb all these fucking stairs; instead, I would have found a good spot in the parking lot out front and crouched down. With a sprightly jump I would fly up and reach the windows on the sixteenth floor. Smashing the glass, I would break into his apartment. I'm lost in a fantasy of wringing the little fucker's neck. But it's of no help when trying to rebuild my body, which has spread out like porridge spilled on the floor. I let out a deep sigh and shoulder my bag—my ball and chain—once more. I have no choice but to continue to climb the stairs.

Around the tenth floor, I start to roar like an animal caught in a trap, almost crawling up the stairs. I've lost my footing. My body is out of control. I think the part of my body that controls balance is totally fucked. Maybe my pores are clogged, but no more sweat comes out, and as my sweat-soaked body dries, a sticky membrane congeals. There are only six floors left. Shit, another six floors is a piece of cake! I am clinging to the hope that the power of suggestion will keep me from breaking down. I don't know what sort of state I'm in. The best way to put it might be that I don't have enough strength left to care. Whatever the case may be, I know from experience that my body is about to puff up like bread in an oven. No mistaking it! My thighs are squirming, trying to poke through my pants and extend themselves. My form is what you'd call a furious wave. Damn it, my pubic area feels stiff. Seems a leg is trying to pop out. The leg I hide in my crotch has the vital

power of a tree root that could crush a boulder. The buttons on my shirt and pants shoot off in all directions like bullets. I am powerless; I can't even keep my own body in check. But I must keep climbing. That bastard must comfort me. No turning back now. How can I even think of turning back when I've struggled to make it this far? It's better to use the strength it'd take to go down to climb up. If I am going to be shaking within an inch of my life, I better be shaking my way to the sixteenth floor. I'm dying of hunger. I want to eat something fresh. I need to stock up. I have to make my way home. I have to see my family. I want to be loved. Starving for love. Won't anybody love . . .

—What's all that racket!

The sudden shout makes me fall flat on my face, nearly impaling my forehead on the corner of a step. My hideously stretched out body meekly curls back up into my clothes like a hermit crab pulling itself into its shell to avoid a predator. My body may be insolent, but it knows how to read a situation. Deeming my monstrous cries excessively loud, a human, who I assume is a middle-aged female, opens her door and steps out into the hall. I lie as still as phlegm hawked onto the street, holding my breath, waiting for her to go back inside. But she is coming closer and closer to the stairwell. She spots me. I look up and see her staring down at me, arms crossed.

—Young lady! What's all this noise? Are you making those sounds?

I can see in her eyes that she wants to believe that no one as beautiful and slender as I am could possibly produce those blood-curling cries. Her eyes tell me that she desperately wants me to hurry up and confirm her beliefs. I have no intention of living up to her expectations, but I don't want to scare her either. I just keep my mouth shut.

—Then where could all that noise be coming from? Did a stray dog get in the building? Well, something strange is going on. Don't you think?

Keeping her arms crossed, she lets out a sigh. Her heart is still beating at a clip. The ripple of air from the sigh hits me. Tiresome creature she is, she pointlessly prattles on, not knowing her words aren't even reaching me as I imagine how fresh her heart would be; how plucking it from her chest and sucking the juices out like slurping a wax candy bottle would give me a big enough boost to make it up the last few flights of stairs. But I must act with caution. There's no reason for me to make a sea of blood by killing this person. If my energy runs out, I can always eat some of the jerky in my bag. Ah, that's right! I completely forgot about the jerky. How could I have forgotten something so important? Thank goodness I refrained from throwing my bothersome backpack out the window! A few moments of quiet later, thinking she had gone inside, I shovel a dozen or so chunks of jerky in my mouth. But then a throat is cleared.

—You don't live here, do you, young lady?

—You're still here?

While still chewing, I shoot a look at her, eyes glinting. She flinches like she's come face-to-face with a bear in the woods and is trying her best to appear calm. I can read her actions so clearly, I almost want to laugh in her face.

—I haven't seen your face around here before.

—I live somewhere else.

—Then do your parents live here? Or are you here to see your boyfriend? What are you doing here? Tell me.

Am I impatient, or is dealing with her becoming more and more annoying? Some humans stick their noses too deep into other people's business, especially when the other person doesn't want them to. At times like this the best course of action would be for both parties to take some deep breaths, don't you think? You never know if one morning your planet will explode, breaking into hunks of rock floating in space with nary a fistful of oxygen for you to suck down. You should breathe it in while you can. Don't be full of regret, like me. Regret isn't a very enjoyable emotion.

—I came here to eat because I'm hungry.

—Oh, are you the daughter of the couple in 1606? You've grown so much! Don't you remember me? I babysat you a couple times when you were little. You don't remember?

—No, I don't.

I stand up quickly and start climbing the cruel stairs again, leaving her mouth gaping at her door.

—What the fuck was that all about? Ah, what a pain, seriously.

Maybe it's because I took a break or because I had a snack, but my body feels so much lighter. I feel like I'm whisking up clouds with my toes. That's an exaggeration, of course. Compared to the days, not long after I landed on Earth, when the pressure of its gravity made even standing still exhausting, these days are like a dream, hahaha.

To my surprise—for it's not often that it works out like this—my body digests the jerky as fast as possible, giving me the energy I need to conquer the remaining stairs. What made it to his front door was not me, but the jerky. The jerky powered through those last five floors. Hooray for jerky! Jerky is the best! I may be a wilted bunch of lettuce, but I remember his request that I not ring the doorbell. Isn't it just so typical? He doesn't want anyone to notice me coming over. Nothing good comes from letting your neighbors know you have an active sex life. Just to piss him off, I could ring that bell a hundred—No! a thousand—times, but won't. All that matters is that I've arrived, and now the long-awaited banquet can begin. Haha, happiness is not long away. To those who've gone through hell, stepping in shit or smelling puke will only make us laugh.

I curl my fingers into a fist, knock softly three times, and wait. Through the door I can hear his heels pounding on the floor as he comes closer. He really must be sex starved. I feel like an owner who's left their puppy home alone while they've gone on a trip. Albeit the only trip I've taken is one up the stairs.

The man from the photos opens the door. He's not too different from the six photos I used to create a 3D image in my mind, if you discount how scruffy he looks and his farmer's tan. And that he seems like he hasn't left his room in days. He too, upon meeting me for the first time, looks me up and down, trying to gauge whether I am worthy of spending time with him.

—Come in. The bathroom's over there.

He points to a door behind him as his eyes—dilating and contracting in a lewd manner—slowly travel the curves clearly visible through my filthy mop of a shirt. Leaving my damp shoes at the door, my exhausted, grubby little feet step into the house. A quick sweep of the room shows me that this is an ordinary apartment. To the left is a small living room with a sofa and TV, and to the right there is a table. The doors leading to the bedroom and the oddly dark bathroom are straight ahead. The two rooms necessary to carry out our—I mean, my—work are pleasantly snuggled up together.

As I pass him, a mélange of scents rises off his skin, and I break them down one by one. A heady mix of odor remover, detergent, shampoo, soap, toothpaste, lotion, rice, kimchi, snacks, and more washes over me in a sensory wave. The fingertips of the hand he used to point out the bathroom door stink of cock. Nasty fucker. While I was killing myself climbing that mountain of stairs, you just sat here playing with your dick, didn't you? If you can't get it up, I'll fucking murder you. No, even if you blow my mind, I'll kill you. You're going to die.

I lock the bathroom door, take off my clothes, and wait for the water to heat up. I brought my bag in with me as well, so I lean it against the toilet. If I hadn't, he might have been curious as to what's inside. And you, dear reader, are the only one who'll get to know what's inside.

The building may look like it's collapsing, but the water pressure is to die for. I might even say it's perfect. I stand in the tub and let the water from the shower head hit me for a long while as clouds of steam billow above me. My body is so listless, I want to abandon my impending plans. I am so tired, and the water is so comforting, that I nearly slough off my vigilance. A bathroom like this is worth one or two more return trips just to freshen up when needed. Mmmmmm, the shampoo and body wash fragrances aren't bad either. However, neither of these scents were coming from his body. Maybe these are products he puts out especially for guests? I'll bet they're the scents he wants to smell on his guests' bodies. It may seem like I'm getting lost in unproductive daydreams, but I have an accurate sense of time and never let the tension in my nerves go slack. If I leave the bathroom in precisely three minutes, I will have enough time to leisurely accomplish my goals.

I hurriedly inspect this female body for defects. It's the ideal body he had described in his profile—down to the letter. I've got to make sure it's a body sure to get him rock solid, a body he'll want to splatter with buckets of cum. In this moment, it's imperative that I am the perfect woman for him, at least corporeally. The Hunter must know the nature of their prey better than anyone else. I towel my hair and dry off my body. Since he said he likes wet hair, I forgo the hair dryer. I intend to satisfy his every desire. It's only polite. My prey's pleasure is my pleasure. If that wasn't the case, why would I be looking into this mirror, reapplying my makeup with such precision?

I exit the bathroom wrapped in only a towel and a cloud of hot, wet air. I hear him calling me sweetly from the bedroom, *Come here*. I'm so thankful, I don't know what to do with myself. He is already completely undressed and is splayed out on the bed, pawing at his dick. He wasn't blowing smoke up my ass. It's truly the king-size organ he said it was. If put to good use, if he really knows what to do, every inch of that column he's erected will give me enormous satisfaction.

The mattress squeaks as the bed rattles in a frenzy. Yes, that's right! We're doing the exact deed you're imagining. You say that you don't even have the slightest inkling as to what I could be doing? You can't read between the lines? Well, then you should do what this man did; send me a message, try and make a date. Make your appeal with your body. Try to bring it upon yourself, try to become my prey. I'm not picky when it comes to faces. They aren't a big deal to me. Well, they are but they aren't. If you happen to have a flat tummy and firm thighs, and the curve of your buttocks is so stunning it could kill, the probability of you receiving the honor of my selection is quite high. No, I'll send the first message. I might even beg and plead, harassing you until I get a reply. However, I will not think twice before eliminating any contenders who live in inaccessible locations. Let's go to a love hotel instead. My treat, naturally. Nothing tops someone who lives on their own near a subway station. Ah, I better stop talking about other things. Please forgive me, but now I must give him my full concentration.

As he does his best, pounding into me, spilling sweat, for over thirty minutes, I imagine he is my adorable lover. We're here to celebrate our three-hundredth day as a couple. My boyfriend has given me a bouquet of flowers and a necklace. And I, of course, have bought him an expensive watch in return. We express our gratitude as we open the gifts, then hug and kiss, until we reach this point. Once we have finished here, we'll run the bath and scatter rose petals over the water. We will get in the tub together, shrieking with laughter as we splash and rub bubbles on one another's nose.

Around lunchtime we'll get out of the bath and dry our hair. Then, taking our time, we'll get ready to go out. We have a reservation for a table by the window at a restaurant known for its impeccable menu. It will be a fabulously elegant meal. Still-blushing steak, cheese salad, and al dente pasta paired with white wine; we eat it all entirely unhurried. We chitchat about how clear the sky is in spring when the rain ends and about the differences between cherry and apricot blossoms. In the end, we don't really know how to tell them apart, and even if we say we do, we promise to forget again by next spring, and we rise from our table and go to the car. Now we are going to view the cherry blossoms and walk off our food along the way. My boyfriend and I each hold an iced coffee in one hand and hold hands with the other. We walk down the path in a storm of white petals falling like snow. The sky is half air, half flowers. As if our sole purpose were to spark envy and inferiority complexes in passersby, we act out the sugary performance permitted only of couples. You measly worms must be dying of jealousy! I'm so happy that it strikes me I'd still be happy if the Earth turned to dust this very minute. I wish it would, so this moment would be preserved forever.

In the split second when something catches my lover's eye, I hide myself. He thinks I'm right behind him. It's a while before he realizes that I've disappeared and, bewildered, he keeps searching for me. At first, he'll think it's a prank, he'll hope it's a prank, but I will not show myself. Little by little, he'll start to worry that I might have been kidnapped. But no woman would be harder to kidnap than me! Or will he think that he's been unexpectedly dumped? No matter how many scenarios he runs through, my boyfriend will never in his life understand my unpredictable act. He'll try his best to comprehend, but the more he tries, the more torturous it will become.

My body cannot endure more than half a day in human form. It's impossible to spend a whole day with my lover, even on a day as lovely as this. My body is like a rubber band. As soon as I step foot outside my house, I stretch it taut. But the more time passes, the more my arms grow weak, and because of its elasticity, the rubber band keeps trying to spring back to its original shape.

My strength has bottomed out. I can no longer perform my duty as his girlfriend. That is to say, the rubber band has snapped my arm.

It would be better for his mental health if he were dating a cherry tree instead. I can't have an ordinary romance with him. Being just friends wouldn't be easy either. To be frank, it's difficult for me to maintain a relationship with any human. There's nothing more troublesome than having to keep disappearing and reappearing. How could you date in that state? Moreover, no one could ever understand my sorry situation.

Can you hear that? It's my boyfriend, searching for me with burning love. If I return to his side right now, he will either run away in fear or throw stones at me. And if that's the worst that happens, it would be a relief because, right now, I look like a triceratops melting in a whirlpool of lava.

He is still teasing me with his body, slick with sweat. He doesn't seem to tire. Impressive. I almost want to applaud. This man, however, hasn't given me a bouquet, and he isn't sucking my nipple because he loves me; he doesn't want to cut my steak up into bite-size pieces and place them into my mouth, nor does he even have the skinniest rat's tail of an intention to hold my hand and look at cherry blossoms. I won't demand anything more from him. We'll casually enjoy ourselves and part ways with no pressure or expectation. All we both need is a living masturbatory aid. All we think is that it would be nice to have a lump of flesh to hold close, rub lips, and mouth our sex organs without all the cumbersome formalities. To brush up against a lump of flesh with an assigned age and gender. Lump of flesh to lump of flesh. That's all. But every now and then, I try to hear love whispered to me by a partner in the hot gusts breathed onto my back or breast. Somehow, I've picked up the habit of trying to sense vibes of love coming from my one-night stands.

I love you. I love you. I love you.

As a matter of fact, a woman I met three months ago had chanted, *I love you*, over and over while eating my ass. She cleaved to my palpitating shithole, turning it into an ear and lips to receive her love. Where on earth was her love going? Who could she have been calling out to, over and over? Did she have business with my small or large intestine? Perhaps she thought that if she screamed *I love you* between my pert parted cheeks, the words would echo back. I think she simply wanted to hear those words—*I love you*. I too want to hear words of love. If yesterday, then today; if today, then tomorrow—I want to hear those words. Even if they are empty lies. Sometimes words, regardless of the sincerity with which they are said, can be a source of ecstatic pleasure in and of themselves. That woman, with such a skillful tongue, was probably looking to feel that ecstasy.

This man, no matter what tricks he pulls, could never

figure out, or even want to know, what I'm thinking about while we fuck. He throws his head back and moans as his cum mercilessly spurts into the condom's reservoir tip. Absentmindedly, I stare at the undulating tendons in his neck. *The Hunter holds their breath.* As a satisfied smile creeps across his lips, I know the time to act is now. He is slowly pulling out, his cock going limp like acorn jelly. *The Hunter sets their sights on their Prey's vital point.* He is probably about to grin and ask, as human males are wont to do, *Was it good for you?* But before the *g* of *good* crosses his lips, I bite his head off. If you saw my teeth, dear reader, you would immediately think of a shark. My razor-sharp teeth penetrate deep into the back of his neck and under his chin. His handsome head breaks free from his spine and slides elegantly down my throat. The taste of his shampoo, lotion, and sweat lingers. Blood fountains from the immaculate slice. I suction my lips to the stump of his neck and greedily drink it all down as his face dissolves in my stomach. The strength of my lips is far superior to that of an octopus's suckers. I can't bear to see any blood drip onto white bedding and leave a stain. Not a single drop of blood may spill. The fact he lives alone, far from his family, is of no consequence; it is imperative that not a single trace remains. And it is such a pain to wash out blood stains.

I lift his body with my mouth, letting it hang like a squid from a drying rack, toes dangling in the air. You've got to let the legs extend fully if you want to suck up even the blood that pools in feet in one go. He's turned white as the driven snow. Now his skin is the same color as in the photos he uploaded. As I always say, you can never trust a profile picture. They're a useful frame of reference, to some degree, but it's nigh impossible to meet someone who matches up exactly with what the photo leads you to imagine. Well, not quite *impossible*.

I shake his legs and swallow, making sure to leave not a single drop of blood behind. All done! I take him out of the bedroom. Step three takes place in the bathroom.

He lies on the floor with his hands laid modestly, one on top of the other. All hair has been removed from his body. He looks a bit incomplete without a head, for some reason. It's a bit awkward to keep calling this body a "he." "It" is more suitable, don't you think, since it's lost the critical elements that it used to form biological bonds and differentiate itself from other humans? It's only human in shape. There are no major differences between it and the carcasses of cows and pigs hanging from hooks in the butcher shop. But humans are still humans when they die. You must be a human when you're dead in order to be accepted as a human when you were alive. To think that it is so easy and natural for them to maintain their humanity when, no matter what I do, it takes so much effort for me to mimic an outward human form for just one day. If possible, I'd love to steal a human body for myself: my forever homework, the thing that would most easily solve the problem of my existence. However, I don't have the power to take someone else's body and make it my own. So instead, as I prepare to break down my kill, I run my hands over every inch and try my hardest to remember the particular anatomy of humans. All I can do is throw myself, heart and soul, into mimesis. To do this, I can't be slapdash and imitate without a logical process. If I must mimic a human, I have to make sure to have an eye-catching figure. People's moods improve at the mere sight of an aesthetically pleasing body. Ah, we'll have to discuss it more later. I have many more people waiting for me on tenterhooks. There's a long day ahead.

I open my bag and take my metal instruments out, one after the other: a set of saws, hammers, and knives as precious as my own limbs. Neat as embroidery stitches, I arrange them on the tile floor in order of size. Just look at the perfect spacing between them, not a millimeter's difference! It calms me; it focuses me. I turn on the cold water and scrub "it" down. The head tastes best when eaten straight away without washing, but I recommend ridding the torso and appendages of any impurities and storing them in the refrigerator for later use. Frying it up in a pan or marinating and braising it are my preferred methods. Take the advice of this gourmand who, these past eleven years, has gorged themselves on any and all types of human flesh.

The cock and balls are a delicacy that must be kept in ice water, then, when ready to eat, sliced fresh like sashimi and dipped in either soy sauce with wasabi or gochujang and vinegar. After I've dragged "it" out of the tub and onto the floor, I carve out the genitals. If you throw the heart, lungs, entrails, and other organs together and boil them in a pot, it's a killer stew, hahaha. Just the thought of it has me drooling. It needs no saying, but you don't have to stick to these same recipes every time you eat. I'm just sharing what I know about bringing out the best of each ingredient. They're also good boiled or fried. Why don't you try your hand at sun-dried jerky?

The butchery begins. With a practiced hand, I sever the joints and debone the meat. Since I've sucked out all the blood, it's easy to immerse myself in the knife work. After I have broken down the human, I slice the meat into hand-span chunks and, using a saw, slice the bones down to size to make human-bone broth. I also smash them into tiny pieces with my hammer. Bone fragments make a great snack—and they'll give your jaw a workout, to boot! And you'll get to taste the marrow. Even the meanest looking of bones hold a savory mouthful.

Since we're on the topic, you'll never believe it, but, at first, I never really thought about eating humans. Never in my wildest dreams did I imagine that I would be out hunting every day. At the time, I had plenty of rations in my cupboard, and I thought that all I would need to do is top up my fuel and be on my way. I haven't fully given up hope of leaving, but the probability is not looking as good as it used to. Looking forward, I know that, chances are, I will be stuck here tomorrow, next week, next month, and even next year. And that's because I've been searching far and wide these past fifteen years but have yet to find any material suitable for fuel. I'm scared I never will. Do I have to take comfort in the fact that my lifespan is four times that of humans? However, the stress of it all may lead me to an early death.

I ran out of food before two months had passed on this planet. To keep from dying of hunger, I threw whatever I could get my hands on down my gullet: tree bark, foliage, dirt, stones, fish, shellfish, moss, lichen, bugs, asphalt, cement, tires, streetlamps, cats, dogs, pigeons, every type of food sold at restaurants, bowls, chair legs, and more. Nothing satisfied my taste buds. Oftentimes, I'd barely hold back retching to swallow it down, and as soon as it hit my stomach, I'd throw it all up. And I was lucky if vomiting was the worst of it. There were many times I succumbed to food poisoning and was incapacitated by high fevers and migraines. I even wished for my life to end, but my body's will to live was so pugnacious that as soon as I'd pass out, my eyes would quickly open again. I limped along like this for four whole years.

Ultimately, I turned my sights on humans. My mind was opened to the prospect of murder! Whereas I once looked upon humans like clouds in the wind or a trail of ants, I began to see things in a different light the longer my hunger set in. I became terribly curious how they might taste. I was consumed with questions: How would I describe their mouthfeel? How would they smell? How rich might their juices be? My instincts screamed at me, insisting that I must eat humans if I want to survive. It seemed I would be able to live a long, healthy life if only I ate humans. I made up my mind that as soon as I stocked up on enough meat and secured fuel, I'd leave this godforsaken planet! The day after I gave myself permission to satiate my hunger with human flesh, I started catching, killing, and ripping apart my prey with no hesitation. Back then, even raw human meat satisfied me. With time came experience, and my methods became more elaborate. I have lived to this day by eating humans. It's not a life without sacrifice. I have to steal human lives to continue my own. I'm sorry. Actually, that apology is a load of shit. It's just a formality, like saying, "How are you?" I'm sorry. I'm sorry. I'm sorry. I love you. I love you. I love you.

I put my, now much heavier, backpack down in the living room and go back to the bedroom. (Don't worry, I left the bathroom spotless.) In front of the full-length mirror,

I pull back my distended facial muscles, which had ac-
commodated harvesting his head, and tuck away my legs,
which had popped out in all the excitement. I pull on my extra panties and clean dress, both giving off the fresh scent
of fabric softener. The way fresh laundry smells never fails
to bring me joy. That is, until my back and crotch get irri-
tatingly damp. I twirl on the spot, then, humming a little
tune, sift through his clothes, looking for his wallet. Where
would he keep it? The inner pocket of his backpack? In
the pocket of a coat hanging in the closet? In the second
drawer? I find it under his sweatpants. It is thin and made
of brown leather—but whose leather? Stuffed inside I find
his ID card, driver's license, business card, credit card,
coupons, receipts, a condom, and four crisp bills total-
ing thirty thousand won. My meat's wallets are my only
source of income. I make about two to three hundred thousand won a day. If I'm lucky, I can make around ten million
won in the span of three hours. Some of the meat even
keep bundles of cash in their homes. I make a pretty good
living, don't you think? In fact, I'm pretty rich. Cash is piled
up in my wardrobe and drawers. I haven't counted, but it
probably adds up to a billion won. I thought long and hard
about whether I should hire a driver, but after considering
the high probability that my secret would be exposed, I decided I'd better not. Anyway, come over some time! I'm so
busy with work that you could steal hundreds and thou-

sands of won, and I'd be none the wiser. There's nothing I could do if I discover I've been robbed. How could I slice you up with my toenail when you're long gone?

Now I'm looking for his phone. I've got to erase all our messages. It's best to delete the apps. Sometimes I smash the phones and throw the pieces away or toss them in the river. Yes, I have completed all my tasks. There's no reason to stay a second longer. Let's hurry on our way. My next appointment is at eleven thirty, so I've got thirty minutes. It's a fifteen-minute trip on the subway. Barely enough time! And no time to rest. My job runs me ragged. Thankfully, the insoles of my sneakers have dried nicely. I wish I could reward them with a treat. I imagine myself smiling down at my sneakers as they excitedly snap up a meaty treat. I grab the door handle when, suddenly, I break out in a cold sweat as a wave of nausea hits me. The hair! I'm struck by these symptoms multiple times a day. I don't know if I'll ever get used to it. Throwing off my bag, I run to the toilet. I'm almost at my limit. My stomach is adamant in its refusal to digest hair; it just won't have it! I don't know if there's anything else it is sensitive to, but hair simply will not do. When my stomach protests so violently, what else can I do but obey. My stomach is my second brain, and sometimes it threatens to steal the top spot. I humbly kneel before the toilet bowl and, without a moan of complaint, cough up two or three clumps of bile-soaked, but otherwise perfectly intact, hair, which bob up, floating in the water. An image of the way he looked when he was alive flashes before my eyes. He truly was a quality specimen. The elevator incident may have soured the mood, but he took care of me in bed. I hope it was a positive experience for him. Mmm, he had a great body, and the sex was great too. Should I have taken him as my twelfth lover? Should I have let him live and serve my sexual gratification? However, I have no lovers that live on the sixteenth floor. That would be ludicrous. What would I do if the elevator was down again, like today? Stairs test the strength and limits of my hunger. Throwing up hair on the sixteenth floor is my punishment for satisfying my craving for fresh head. Ah, I've got to hurry now! Going on about "sixteenth floor this, sixteenth floor that" is going to give me a fear of heights.

I check to make sure I've locked the door. I sense a suspicious presence behind me, and whipping around— almost snapping my neck—I discover a forty-something-looking man staring at me. The shock of an unexpected human appearing shot my eyes off in opposite directions, like a snail's stalks, and I have to work to pull them back to the center of my face. I waste a minute and a half trying to pull his face into focus. It's a waste of precious time, but I don't know if this man might attack me. You've got to see clearly if you're going to face your enemy head-on. I pull my body tight like a bowstring to summon my toenail and horn at a moment's notice. Are you going to mock me for being too sensitive? Sensitivity is essential for protecting yourself. Maintaining this knife's edge every minute, every second of the day is better than dying and disappearing without a trace. It's thanks to my sensitivity that my body has managed to survive until now. Without it I would have been knocked flat out hundreds of times.

—Who are you?

—And who are you, sir?

—As you can see, I live across the hall.

He gestures rudely at the door. Who asked? That's obvious.

—I didn't know the young man who lives here has a girlfriend.

—I'm not his girlfriend.

—Then you're . . . ?

—I'm his brother. I mean his sister. Si-i-s-ter.

Would it have been better to just let him think I'm his girlfriend? Getting dragged into this old man's bullshit puts a nasty taste in my mouth. There's nothing like an interrogation to ruin your mood. But I'm sitting here giving unimpeachable answers. My mouth moves on its own.

—I thought he was an only child . . .

—Well, he isn't.

—Oh, is that so? Well, how's your brother doing? I haven't seen him around in a while. Has he been sick?

—He's doing *juuuuuuust* fine.

I stretched out my reply like a yawn. Trying to get across in tone alone that I'm through with this conversation. I'm not sure if he got it. I'm still working on communicating like a human. However he understood it, it seemed to have some sort of effect. After sneaking a peek at my thighs, exposed by my short dress, he seemed to lose interest and turned to the elevator, which was now back to work. I wonder what he'd taste like if I bit off his pointing arm? As I admire the veins bulging on his forearm and back of his hand, I calculate how much damage my schedule would take if I dropped my next appointment and took a tumble in the elevator with this old man.

The doors slide open, and I follow him into the elevator, shaking my head. However, that did nothing to shake the curiosity swarming my mind. Quite the opposite, it threw me deeper down the rabbit hole, so much so that I can't even enjoy my comfortable elevator ride down from the sixteenth floor. I imagine how he might taste. The sound of his breathing feels so close, I can clearly hear the sound of him smacking his lips and swallowing. His eyes drink me in as he reaches peak arousal. I can say with confidence that if I grab his hardened penis and stick my tongue between his lips, he will not hesitate to grab

my tits. Unfortunately, the elevator stops on the eleventh
floor. Did I say unfortunately? Am I that put out about being unable to jump his bones?

—Oh, we meet again, young lady.

The woman I ran into on the eleventh floor comes between us. She always does the most annoying thing. Since
it's turned out this way, should I just kill the both of them?
No, no. I should actually be grateful. Thanks to her exquisite intervention, I will be able to complete my schedule as
planned. I don't know what got into me. Taking a second
look at him, this old man probably lives with his wife and
daughter, and if I mess with someone like that, I'd be asking for trouble. The perfect way to get caught. The police
will enthusiastically interrogate me. They could even figure out where I live. As soon as my identity is exposed, it's
the end for me. The last curtain-call. I will probably have
to wrap up my life on Earth. And I can't let myself forget about the security camera perched up in the corner of
the elevator. I could change my face, but that's easier said
than done—creating a new face takes incredible precision.
What's difficult is making a face that performs all its nor-
mal functions while also looking natural and beautiful—
it's not as easy as planting a seed and having beans grow!
And worst of all, this face is my precious new model and
has barely been used yet. It'll break my heart if I have to

throw it away after only a few days. I must avoid situations that call for my face to be destroyed at any cost.

—Why haven't you answered me?

—Excuse me?

—I said, where are you off to dressed so pretty, carrying a big backpack like that? What's in the bag? It looks really heavy.

Ugh, not again. The best course of action is not to respond when you're faced with a busybody who loves nothing more than to stick their nose into other people's business. Maybe it's because my personality hasn't warped yet, or maybe it's because, when adapting to human society, I was forced to master etiquette as a matter of necessity, I can't help but to answer her.

—It's none of your concern. (Before I kill you.)

To tell the truth, having someone not reply and treat me as a nonentity is a teeth-chatteringly frightening experience. There are so many people who ignore someone as naturally as eating. I've seen so many guys like that, and I make sure to keep a mental record of each and every one of their ugly mugs. Answering human leeches like her is almost like a reflex for me, probably because the violence of going unanswered has cut me to my core.

—Don't you agree?

She turns to the old man after I give her my unenthu-
siastic reply.

—Well, seeing a pretty little slip of a thing like her with
a big old bag like that. . . . It just doesn't look right, does it?

—Ah ha ha, I guess that's true.

She continues spewing nonsense until the elevator
reaches the ground floor. All that yammering must be
murder on her muzzle. He darts out of the elevator as soon
as the doors open.

—Ma'am?

I grab her sleeve. The elevator doors slowly creak shut.
Her eyes open wide.

—You said you wanted to know what could possibly be
in my big ol' bag, didn't you?

I use the sweetest, most bubbly tone I can muster.

—Ah, well, I'm actually really busy right now . . .

—Where do you think you're going?

I wrinkle my face in places that won't fuck it up and
show her my teeth. My back is to the security camera, so
I don't have to worry about my true form getting caught.
Unable to make a sound, she watches as I dig around in my
bag. She's totally lost her mind. I place a chunk of meat in
her hanging jaw.

—Bye-bye, now!

I press the open button. She doesn't seem like she
wants to get off the elevator anymore. As the doors close, I

see her retching and heaving, as she spits out the present I left in her mouth. She only gets out of the elevator as I exit the building. With a spring in my step, I walk toward the subway station thinking of the humans who eagerly await my call.

* * *

I have c o m p l e t e d my day's work. I am so w o r n o u t that I wouldn't b e s u r p r i s e d if my head r o l l e d off and my arms and legs crumbled to pieces, but since I have a m p l e f o o d in my bag and t h e s u n s e t is so r a v i s h - i n g my body c a n ' t h e l p b u t d a n c e. My house is d e e p in a forest on the outskirts of the city. D e e p i n t h e w o o d s where visitors rarely tread. No one shows up at my house. The s t r a p s of my bag are digging into my shoulders and just might s l i c e my arms clean off! As I a m p u s h e d f o r w a r d by the weight of my bag, I s e e t h e p i n k s k y through the leaves—my s i d e - e f f e c t - f r e e a n e s t h e t i c — and take it all in. All too s o o n i t i s p e n e t r a t e d by the night. I a m a l m o s t h o m e. My house looks like a p i l e o f h a p h a z a r d l y stacked boxes; g r e e n a n d o r a n g e, with soft glints of dusty silver and gold. And n o m a t t e r w h e r e I may be, if it senses me, it d a r t s o u t i t s tongue of beaming r e d r a y s and snatches me up, p u l l i n g my body inside. Sometimes it leaves me reeling, as if my thoughts have been left behind.

The light hanging from the cavernous ceiling switches on, and as soon as I set down my bag, I strip, throwing off my clothes and shoes. Finally liberated! Like branches stretching out as a tree matures, my body unfurls itself. The makeup caked on my face cracks and falls off. My head expands. Hair spreads out in all directions, filling every nook and cranny. My eyes slide down like raw eggs! It's as if a rainbow were slung between the boughs.

My skin is rough like a dinosaur's, with red spots stamped on a yellow base. The hair covering my body is blue as the morning sky, and my eyes, like two full moons, push through to view the glittering world. And on my forehead is a jet-black shield made of bone studded with horns, which if I used all my strength, could take down two or three humans. But I mostly use it to bash out my stress by thrusting it into tree trunks in the forest. When the birds fly away and the leaves fall like rain, it really lifts my spirits.

I have three legs, and one arm on my right side. Actually, if you look at them as a human would, it

is an arm, but to me it is not a t r u e   a r m ,   b u t   a fourth leg. So that makes the b u m p   c u r v e d like a hook what you humans would call a toenail. A h ,   b u t   there aren't any toenails on m y   f i r s t ,   s e c o n d , and t h i r d l e g s . On the u n d e r s i d e of my feet are slippery t u n - nels   f r o m   w h i c h   offspring s l i d e   out. (Sometimes I send out clots of b l o o d   like rotten milk from here as well.) Have y o u   g o t t e n   t h e   g i s t   of what I look like? I am a being that always requires f r i e n d l y   explana- tion. If I d o   n o t   e x p l a i n , no one understands me. Only beings l i k e   m y s e l f   must p r o v i d e   e x p l a - n a t i o n . The demanding you; the demanded of me. You are the d e f a u l t   l i f e - f o r m . You are the c e n t e r   o f the universe. It must be s o 0 O 0 o 0 O 0 o 0 O 0 o nice.

I throw my s w e a t - s o a k e d   c l o t h e s   into the wash. The washing machine r e m o v e s   the skin-scum from the clothes a n d   d i r t i e s   i t s e l f . I take my b a - b i e s   out of my bag, p l a c e   t h e m   i n   t h e   s i n k , and scrub them squeaky clean. I must e x t r i c a t e   any remaining scraps of flesh c a u g h t   b e t w e e n   t h e t e e t h   of my saws. My babies m u s t   f o r g e t what they've done. O n e   b y   o n e , they enter the u l - t r a v i o l e t   sanitizer and f a l l   into an a m n e s i a c sleep. Now the man from r o o m   1605 shyly crawls out, bit by bit. I throw the refrigerator d o o r s   w i d e o p e n . His rightful place is n o   l o n g e r   the bedroom,

but here. About h a l f   o f   h i m will be frozen and wh at
remains will be kept well chilled. His cock and balls
take their s p e c i a l   p l a c e in the refrigerator's to p m o s t
d r a w e r. They have c e r t a i n l y   e a r n e d that right.

After washing out my water bottle, c l e a r i n g
away the half-e a t e n jerky, and r e a r r a n g i n g
any remaining c l o t h e s   a n d   m a k e u p, it is time to
s a y goodbye to my bag. N o w   i t   i s   m y   b o d y ' s   t u r n to
be cleaned. My body is t i r e d from d o i n g   i t s   b e s t
today. We have a l o v e - h a t e —no, a love-h a t e - h a t e -
h a t e —relationship, but if I am going to coax and cajole
it into p e g g i n g away again tomorrow, I   m u s t   t r e a t
i t with the u t m o s t devotion. It's hard to g e t   i t   t o
w o r k if it starts to sulk. I take myself into the bathroom,
d r a g g i n g my body like a tired, old, feral dog. I
s i n k   i n t o the tublike toilet / toilet-like-tub. W i t h   t h e
press of a button, hot water c a s c a d e s   o v e r   m e,
and once I'm fully submerged, the h o l e s in my skin
open up, and s h i t (mixed with piss) trickles out
like s w e a t. Nine million of these little pinecone-like
forms p u s h   o u t and plip-plop into the water, where
they d i s s o l v e. They are the dregs left behind from
the five h e a d s I s w a l l o w e d today. D i r t y water is
f l u s h e d   a w a y, and clean w a t e r   r e f i l l s
in succession. O n   t h e   f i n a l   r o u n d, a heady, per-
fumed foam p o u r s   o u t. Then a warm, dry breeze.

A h h , my body is so relaxed it h a r d l y k n o w s what to do with i t s e l f . Now that it has been d i s a r m e d , my body is much e a s i e r to deal with. I even m a n - a g e to softly toss it onto the bed. T h e t i m e h a s c o m e f o r s l e e p . I ask the h o u s e to wake me up at 2:45 p.m. The house turns off the lights and turns on the television. I wrap myself in the human chatter and misty glow and tuck myself in.

Y a p Y a p Y a p Y a p Y a p Y a p Y a p Y a p .

It feels like I am not alone. Although, i t w o u l d b e s o n i c e if someone would c o m e t o m y s i d e and hold me tight. I f t h e y s t a y at least until I fall asleep, I w o n ' t m i n d if they leave. T e a r s d r i b - b l e down my face as I fall a s l e e p , r u b b i n g and soothing the sex organs hanging from my sides and t w o c r o t c h e s , e q u a l l y , like a bird f e e d i n g its young.

A planet
EXPLODES
!!!

Shards of glass spray in my face. Out of my mind, I launch the spaceship. The air burns. My home is engulfed in flames. Where is my family? Where are my lovers? Where are my friends? Where am I? Dozens of enemy vessels fire at me. The hull is hit by laser strikes and shakes violently.

The shields are of no use. These ships are the ones that destroyed the planet I lived on. Why? Tell me why! What reason do you have for snatching away the foundations of my life? What right do you have? Who could ever replace such a peacefully mundane life? Am I left to live all on my own? Have all others like me been wiped out? Impossible to tell. Right now, nothing is certain. The only thing I can do is use all my remaining strength to escape my death. Escape is the only way to live. Ughaaaahhhhhh! The ship begins to spiral. The needle on the fuel gauge drops lower and lower. Save me! Save me! Save me! Save me! Save me! Save me! Please . . .

I wake up after a night of f i t f u l , t h r a s h i n g sleep. I kick off the c l a m m y , s w e a t - s o a k e d blanket. I have to g e t a g r i p on my startled heart. One d e e p breath, two d e e p breaths. Every night, without exception, I am plagued by nightmares. No, not plagued by dreams but by my past. There is n o w a y t o b r e a k f r e e from its grip. T h e p a s t is a discarded thread of s p i d e r silk. If I am not careful, I could spend my whole life unknowingly w r a p p e d u p in it. But the more a w a r e I become of the spider silk, the more tightly it will bind me. Then I see a v i s i o n of a spider c h a r g i n g down the thread straight at me. What I have just seen is a h a l l u c i n a t i o n . But you have to know it is a hallucination in order to identify it as a hallucination. That's why these visions are often more terrifying than reality. Even as I mumble to myself, *I've got to d r y o u t my blanket, I've got to hurry up and a i r i t o u t in the sunlight*, I drift back to sleep ...

Brrrrr
rrrrr
rrrr

Thanks to the house v i b r a t i n g itself, I wake up right on time. M y b l a n k e t has now dried to a crisp. I sit my n a u s e o u s body up and s t r e t c h . A re-freshing start to the day. Must I o n c e a g a i n o p e n your eyes to the fact that I have not two legs, but t h r e e ? I undulate them like a r i p p l e o v e r w a t e r as I head to the bathroom where I bash out a k a l e i d o - scopic morning w a n k . It isn't really mor n i n g now, but that's what I call it. My orgasm briefly w a s h e s a w a y suffering. Everyone, please masturbate! A l t h o u g h , there are times when self-p l e a s u r e o n l y l e a d s to m o r e p a i n . After washing away my suffering, I amble through to the living room where the pi-lot seat stands. (My suffering starts to l a y e r i t s e l f l i k e c o a t s of dust in preparation for w h a t i s t o c o m e .) I go to the kitchen, press the taupe wall, and let in warm sunbeams and a breeze. There are no windows in my house. No, that's not quite right: there are no fixed windows. Any wall you open becomes a window. The house can be fully lit just with electric lights, but electric lights don't give off any warmth. Not to mention, electric lights also provide neither a spring breeze nor a forest view.

Smacking my lips, I open the refrigerator and take out a hunk of thigh meat, season it generously, deftly sear it in a hot pan, and plate it up. I sit down on a plush gray chair, and start to eat, blowing on my bites to cool them off. And as per usual, I turn on my curved screen and log on to the dating apps. Yippee! Today, as always, there are countless people proudly displaying their bodies. Shall we take a closer look? What gets me the most excited is leisurely examining the quality of the meat in the display case—its look and size. This meat only exists in my self-satisfied imagination as of yet, and like a snowball rolling down a hill, as its destiny unfolds, it'll grow bigger and bigger—this meat will be delicious! And it'll be all the cuter and sexier because of it. What a joy it is to be conned. That is if you never catch on. I grab the joystick with my toenail and continue to scan through the profiles. They put so much effort into turning me on; they try to explain themselves, or misrepresent themselves, or hide themselves through all manner of angles and lighting. I collect the photos, videos, and self-introductions they upload and deliberate who I will send a message to. Characteristics of utmost importance are the quality of the meat, their level of experience, if they live alone, and if they are inclined to go to a motel. And as for distance, I never make contact with people outside my 70 km range. It is such a pain to travel to any destination beyond it. To not take into account the amount of energy consumed by riding the subway would be unprofessional.

Ah, there is a pretty good-looking woman (or so I assume) about 21 km away. Their screen name is L i v 3 A l 0 n 3. They haven't posted their age, but they appear to be in their mid-thirties. There are no pictures of their face, just shots that highlight their tits and ass. Height: 179 cm, weight: 83 kg. For some unknown reason, I am drawn to this rhinoceros. They've even written, "You think you can handle this?" in their profile. I tell myself that I can certainly handle them as I select one of my six profiles to send a message from.

Hunting4luv: Hiya~
Liv3AlOn3: Hello.

Hunting4luv: You DTF?

Liv3AlOn3: I'm kind of busy today . . .

Hunting4luv: How about tomorrow?

Liv3AlOn3: I'll be at home.

Hunting4luv: Does tomorrow at 6:15 p.m. work for you?

Liv3AlOn3: Ah, yeah, that works. So . . . how old are you?

Hunting4luv: I'm 28. And you?

Liv3AlOne: I'm 34.

Hunting4luv: Okay, so where do you live?

I pull up my schedule and add the date. I add an abbreviated version of our conversation so as not to get my hookups confused. I also attach their photos. A receipt for my order. I will go to pick it up at its appointed time. A h , in the time it took to set this date up, I have forty-one new messages. So many of you drooling over my delectable visage. Most of you aren't even fit to judge me. You're underweight or old and decrepit. Cheap cuts. Even if you're handed to me, I won't eat you. I'll still turn up my nose if you arrive kneeling on a silver platter. You are nothing but gluttons for my time. I survey all of their requirements and, comparing them all, decide who I'll message and who I won't. Now that I've seen to the administrative work, I have a little free time left before making my commute, so after I wash the dishes and

vacuum, I'll either h a n g   t h e   l a u n d r y out to dry
or make some jerky. Sometimes, I climb onto the r o o f
and indulge in a spot of sun and forest b a t h i n g . It may
be hard for you to believe, but t h e r e   a r e   e v e n   t i m e s
when precious little birds perch and chirp on my shoulders. It seems like t h e y   t h i n k   o f   m e as a moving
tree branch. There is g o o d   s u n l i g h t today, so I'll
put some meat in t h e   d r y i n g   b a s k e t .

The time is 4:59 p.m. In order not to be late, I have
to stop fiddling with the meat and reconstruct my
flesh. There is a full-length mirror, a vanity, and an
e n o r m o u s wardrobe in the living room. I stand in
front of the mirror for thirty minutes, sweating heav-
ily as my body turns to a moldable dough and I
make my initial form. I shrink my eyes a n d   d r a g
t h e m   u p w a r d ; pop out a nose bridge; decrease
the capacity of my mouth; trim my teeth to a rectangle
shape and slot them into a straight line; take out
earflaps near my temple; match the location and number
of my arms, legs, and genitals to the hu-
man body; adjust the texture of my skin; p u l l   b a c k
the blue fur covering my body
until it remains only on top of my head, in my armpits, and
my pubis and turn it black; and suck in my yellow skin
and red spots until only one remains as a beauty
mark under my eye. Now my eyes act, not inde-

pendently, but in unison, making sure they are blinking at the same time. After all this time, I still forget to blink and get confused. But it is better to leave my eyes wide open than to blink with alternating eyes, however terrifyingly snakelike I may seem.

I drink in my dazzling reflection in utter satisfaction. A chubby, pale, twenty-one-year-old male flashes a dimpled smile back at me. He is all hot and bothered thinking about meeting the woman ten years his senior who calls him a sex pig. Today is the last day they will meet. Is the piggy finally ready to leave the pen? No. Not at all. There's not even the slightest possibility. If he thought he could leave as light and fresh as he is now, he's made a deep miscalculation. He has to cover his body in pieces of cloth! But before he can do that, he must practice walking again. I can't lose focus for a second, even if it is a body I have used tens of times before. Because when I calm my nerves and relax at home, my body will immediately return to its original—balanced and harmonious—state. To regulate my body properly in front of others, I need to put myself through repeated excruciating training. This is my survival strategy. It would be wonderful if my body understood my objectives. No, I know that it is deliberately ignoring them. It hasn't been that long since reconstructing

them, but my arms and legs writhe and wriggle, letting me know they don't want to leave the house. What a ball ache.

I start my practice with pushing each leg forward in turn while shifting my center of gravity. Once I feel safe walking on flat ground, I go up the iron stairs installed along the wall of the living room. To use stairs properly, I must practice standing and holding my weight on one foot. Every time I set foot on stairs, I feel like I am circling the slippery lips of a predator. Stairs are my nemesis. Of that I can assure you. This piggy held tight to the handrail and walked backward down the stairs. With all this practice, I might even be better at climbing stairs than humans. It is a lovely, clear spring day, so I will be able to flit about like a sparrow. I run to the wardrobe, pull out my underwear and clothes, and get dressed. I embody my date's exact taste in men. For her, I have created a man worthy of playing between her legs. I double check if my skin has the right texture; if the ratio of my nose, eyes, and lips is correct; if my arms, legs, and body are symmetrical; if my nipples are level; if my dick is the same shape as last time; and if my leg is crouching sweetly beneath my pubic hair. Perfection! This little piggy will once again completely fool their date. Dear reader, I am no longer the woman that you knew. The only thing that hasn't changed is my drab hiking backpack. All my tools, airtight containers, jerky, water bottle, towel, toothbrush and toothpaste, shampoo, lotion, perfume, condoms, lube, makeup, panties, clothes, accessories, and shoes are inside. Have I kept you waiting too long?

Let's go!

The house spits me out onto the hardened earth. Keeping my eyes closed, I allow the shadows of the leaves to flutter on my face to their heart's desire. I walk through the forest, taking deep breaths of fresh air. I feel so refreshed I want to show it off. I don't know if I've ever felt gravity pressing down on me just right as I do right now. If I keep feeling like this I just might float away, hahaha. But I get ahold of myself. I've decided this is enough. Happiness is an incredibly rare and dangerous emotion. I'm someone who can't bear the fall from happiness to despair. I need a safety net to prepare for it since the higher I climb, the greater my injuries will be when I fall. That's what's so frightening. You never know when an iron mace will beat you out of your drunken happiness, casting you into hell. Am I incapable of fully enjoying even the smallest moments of happiness? As soon as I'm happy, I start having ominous thoughts of ruining that happiness.

A couple of people in comfortable clothing show up. They make a line heading in the direction of the forest lodge. I try my best to walk slowly and stay as far away from them as possible but find that I look like I'm following the tail end of the line, and for some reason, it darkens my mood. If only I had a small axe in my hand, the family of four walking in front of me, laughing, chatting, and stinking of sweat, would get chopped up like firewood. I think that would lift my spirits a notch or two. I must apologize. I can't explain why I sometimes fantasize about massacring humans without any rhyme or reason. Is it because I want to pass the responsibility for my unhappiness on to them? Whose fault is it that I'm unhappy? Is it a problem I can only solve on my own? Without knowing what sort of mood I am walking through this forest in, they keep flapping their lips, trying to speak to me, but I'm in a precarious state where engaging me in conversation might endanger their lives. No, I've got to cut in front of these fucking maggots before I crush them under my feet.

The station is swarming with maggots too. I can't find a seat and am being pushed here and there, getting squashed up against the train doors, staring dazedly at the mass of maggots reflected in the window. I can't even secure a spot to set my bag down for a bit. Now that I think about it, I've taken the subway at rush hour. I am stone dead. Is happiness merely a mirage? Is it a rainbow that disappears as suddenly as it appears? An unstable cloud that looks like it might shortly burst. That's the state I'm in. My gums ache and itch. My teeth are ripping at my cheeks, screaming to be let out. I hold my shuddering mouth shut with two hands. My eyeball threatens to slide behind my right ear, and my left leg bends backward like a deer's. Haha . . . what a mess. I become the focus of the other passengers' gazes. They whisper to each other, *Look over there, what's wrong with that person, so weird, I'm scared.* Hello, everyone? I can hear you all. Let me tell you, my hearing is perfectly sharp, even if my earlobes are dripping onto my shoulders.

As soon as the doors of this not-coffin open, I totter off in search of the toilets (although I wish I could run), swinging my arms that have stretched and bloated like overcooked noodles. I feel like a food waste bag dripping its rotten soup. I'm in a jam. People are busy avoiding me up close and pointing at me from afar. My gait has quickly become the object of ridicule and horror. Am I wrong? It would be great if I was. I understand their hearts, a hundred, a thousand times over. For them, life is so boring that if someone doesn't walk with ease, taking steady steps on two healthy legs of the same length, they violently overreact as if they were waiting for it. I think their bar for reactions is pretty low. They can't wait to ogle a monster. Without monsters, how would they withstand the unrelenting futility of their days?

I am stamping my squishy feet in front of the bathrooms. For the fucking life of me, I can't figure out which one I've got to go in. I blindly follow where my feet take me. What luck! I sigh in relief at the sight of the urinals. No one is screaming or shouting at me to get out. No one slaps me across the face! In the men's bathroom, they only focus on pissing or taking a shit.

I hurry into a cubicle, lock the door, and set my bag down on top of the toilet lid. Ordinarily, I can incorporate the knowledge I have gathered, memorized, and internalized these past ten years without a hitch, but when I'm thrown off guard like before, I collapse like a sandcastle defenseless against the tide. Why can't I blend in naturally with groups of humans? Won't someone kindly share the secret? Can I become a human and receive love? Is that too much to ask for? Ah, it's fine now. Please, don't worry about it. Pay it no mind. You'll all say that I don't know what beat to follow, and if I'm crazy, I'm solidly crazy. But, dear reader, don't you know it all too well? Know that if you aren't crazy, at least once, there will come a time in your life when you simply cannot bear it. A time when it's hard to tell exactly what trips your madness. I have some good news for you. I've safely made it through that time. As soon as the tides roll back, I can rebuild the sandcastle. I pull the corners of my mouth into a forced expression of enjoyment. I whistle as I stand in front of the sink. I've got to get this little piggy to her in one piece, haha! Her tender greeting rings in my ears, *You cute little* . . . I splash some water on my forehead and neck to wash away the sweat before heading out.

When walking down the stairs, human heads fill my view, bobbling like berries, but when going up the stairs, I run my eyes over the calves of the people in front of me as if hugging a puppy. They look like sausages with their casings peeled off. With every step they climb, this calf wibbles and that calf wobbles. It's like they're whispering, *Bite me, gobble me up*. I want to sever the limb at the knee and slice through the ankle so I can eat it in one bite, pulling the perfectly cleaned bone from my lips. A flavor simply to die for! I keep on living thanks to you guys helping me forget how laborious it is to climb the stairs. As I traverse the transfer station, I think of her calves. They're a bit on the short side. Although, I am quite grateful that they are nice and toned, making them all the better to rip from the bone. Stepping on the bumpy yellow panels that mark the path, I quickly find my way to the right platform.

While we're waiting for the train, how about we move the conversation on from calves? During the week, she is an office worker who keeps her nose pressed to the grindstone, and the words *I'm tired* are always on the tip of her tongue. A rotten smell of cigarettes and coffee oozes from her mouth. She tries to hide it with mouth deodorizing spray, but there's no fooling my nose. That's why, whenever we kiss, I only breathe through my mouth. Today, before I kill her, I absolutely must tell her the truth. It'd be such a shame for her to die without knowing that she's spewing poison gas from her kisser. I want to give her the most beautiful demise possible. All because, even though she's been endlessly demanding in bed, this woman is so extraordinarily skilled in her caresses that she makes my eyes roll back in my head. In her eyes, I'm so cute and squishy that she just wants to pop me in her mouth like candy. She has treasured and cared for me as if I were her own brother. There's no way that being taken care of can feel this warm and good. Of course, she was mostly taking care of herself. I'm nothing more than a plaything stuck between the two sides of her. It's the same for her. She, too, is stuck between me and myself. We are two interlocking circular saw blades. We've been meeting up once or twice a month for the past year. I have been trying to break free from this cycle. My reasoning is simple. She bores me. I'm sure I bore her and annoy her too. Her plan is just to keep me around until she finds another partner.

Like dough, I hang from a strap in the train. It seems it's my fate to never get a seat today. As long as the handle doesn't snap, there won't be any incident ending in me disgustingly sprawled out on the floor, but . . . it really isn't fair that I can't pop out an extra leg. With three legs I could prop myself up as steady as a tripod. I don't think I'll ever be able to practice enough to erase how unstable I feel on two legs.

I wasn't raised as a life-form of limited imagination. But truthfully, on my home planet, no one could have imagined that there is something that walks around on two legs swinging its two arms. The idea of it must have been tossed around at some point, but we would be hard pressed to believe that bipedalism was *really* possible and that there really is a whole group of life-forms out there somewhere living on two legs. On my planet, we have no trouble balancing on four legs, or on three legs with one arm. After getting a leg cut off in an accident, just a few days' rest will restore their number back to what it was before. While trying to live in this place, it feels like I am forced to amputate a leg and have a transplant surgery to make it into an arm. It kind of feels like I'm dough being pressed through a cookie cutter and baked till crisp.

My knees start to ache. It's not a lie. I'm in pain, I tell you. My body is slowly approaching the point where it's difficult to pretend that I am okay. If I didn't keep my body tightly restrained, I wouldn't even last ten minutes. There's no way to prove how feeble I am. I can't hang around with the old people or concoct some excuse to shoo the young people out of their seats. This is because my body looks to be the picture of health until right before it reaches the point of being cruelly beyond repair. So why don't you pretend to be an old person and get to have a seat for your whole ride, you say? No, I don't want to commit such a foolish act. It would be even more wasteful of my energy. Remodeling my body is not as easy as flipping over your hand. Our species originally used its transformative powers as a last resort when escaping a dangerous situation, like a lizard cutting off its tail; but unlike an octopus that can change its shape and color at will, we must endure the pain of breaking bones that accompanies our transformations. I simply can't waste this power on frivolous luxuries like sitting on the subway. I've got to take my chances to make a successful kill and fill my belly, my fridge, and my larder. Or to take the chance to feel warmth through physical touch with another. That's why I'm fully prepared to withstand whatever tortures the subway has for me as long as I can easily sustain myself for the day. And, of course, I'd never dream of overpacking my schedule. The number of times I can change my body in a day is pretty much set. My ability to transform depends on what condition my body is in. I follow its lead when making these decisions. My body has a mind of its own and is constantly screaming for independence. It would probably get along just fine without me.

On the other hand, it's not like old people always get seats. If the train is crammed with people, they too have no choice but to stand. Just like me. As humans age, they naturally become more and more like me. Often, I observe the elderly push people's backs and cut in line in order to grab a seat and see them struggling alone as they try to hang on to the handrail when going up or down stairs. I feel a strange camaraderie with them. Every once in a while, I see myself in them. They are much younger than me but sometimes seem to struggle as much as I do. Although, once, an old guy shoved me to the floor and gleefully stomped all over me, all the while saying I had invaded "his" seat. I recognize them, but they do not recognize me. It's a shame, but it's okay. An old person couldn't stomp me to death. I have to keep a tight hold of myself because even my gentlest prod could send them all the way to hell. You say that good things come to those who wait? Nothing good comes, but I keep waiting.

—Take a seat.

Some kind of angel gets into an awkward position, intending to offer me their seat.

—I'm fine.

I spit out the habitual response in spite of myself. I'm worried they'll take my nonsensical reply at face value. Not a single part of me is fine.

—Take a seat. Your bag looks heavy.

Thanks to their chivalry, I can gently lower my buns. Is this my good karma coming back to me? When the train stops, my angel flits out the doors like a sparrow. Thank you! For once the words aren't merely lip service. Once again, I give thanks. I shut my eyes. A ray of golden light strokes both of my cheeks. The leaves are fluttering, and my lungs fill with fresh air. Somehow I'm now in a densely packed forest. Not a single person is there. *Coo coo coo coo coo.* Pigeons hop from branch to branch, crying out as if giving orders. I am at peace. The feeling spreads through me to the tips of my fingers and toes. Here my day starts anew. Sometimes you just need to start off on the right foot, get your buttons fastened right. I drag my now pleasantly puttied body out of the train and set my foot on the first step of the stairs and my hand on the railing.

My phone vibrates. She's calling me. I'll answer it, and before I can even say hello, she'll immediately ask me where I am.

—Where are you?

My mind sharpens. Her steely voice has a rousing power. I might even say it's as if someone has shoved a finger in my ear.

—I'm almost there.

—Okay, hurry up. I miss you.

She uses those words as easy as eating. She's already lying under the covers, wearing nothing but her panties, hungrily waiting for me. I can see it clearly. When I crack open the door and shyly peek around the corner, she'll be lying on her side, propping up her head, and saying, *Is that my sweet little piggy? I'll buy you something nice to eat after. Let's have a good time today.* I take off my backpack and set it on top of the cheap table, then, snorting, take off my clothes. She's burning holes with her eyes as she looks my naked body up and down from the fat little titties protruding from my chest, to my milky white belly, to my dingle-dangling dick. Mirroring the naivete that arouses my prey, I avoid making eye contact with her and feign hesitation as I open the glass door to the bathroom. Returning after my shower, I keep up the act in vain as I crawl beneath the blankets. Doing exactly as she wants, I pull her panties down to her ankles and get to work licking and sucking her wet cunt. My tongue becomes five thick eels that quickly seek out her depths. She'd never dream of what shape her partner's tongue has just taken. She simply can't afford to. Could anyone ever compete with my technique? With only one tongue it'd be impossible.

Now then, on to the next step. As her breath quickens, she whispers, *Ah, please, stop,* just before she reaches the peak of her pleasure. And then she pushes at my roasted tomato red face. I pucker my lips like an octopus sucker and, with a smacking kiss, pull back. I come out of the blankets, pull my arms to my chest, and lie down on my belly. If she pinches, bites, and spanks my ass, then tickles my back with her tongue, I'll respond with a stream of

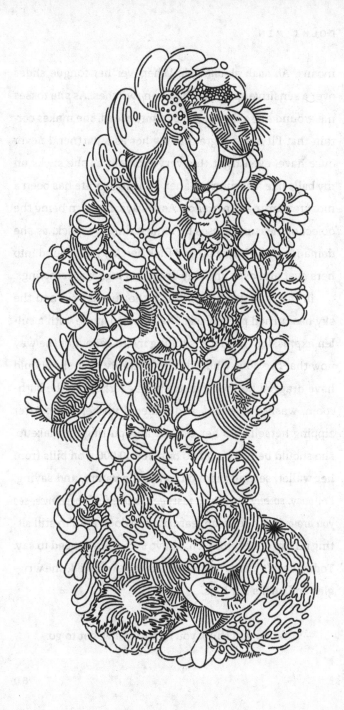

moans, *Ah aaah ah ahhh ah*. Whenever her tongue slides over a sensitive spot, my abdomen twitches. As she tosses me around like a fluffy slice of white bread, she makes certain that I'll never regret having her as a partner. I never once have, even right this very moment as she sucks on my balls like a vacuum cleaner. Sparing her life has been a most rewarding experience. As always, my turn being the object of pleasure passes by almost unfairly quick, as she demands that I hurry up and fuck her. My hips pound into hers over and over until my arms and legs are trembling.

In the time it takes to finish, the sun has set and the sky has turned pitch black. She looks up at me with a sullen expression. Her face is telling me to get out of the way now that I've done what I'd come to do. By now, she should have dragged her body, heavy with exertion, to the bathroom, washed her hair, and lathered up her body. After zipping herself into her clothes and putting on makeup, she should be plucking two or three 10,000 won bills from her wallet, setting them on top of the vanity, and saying, *I'm busy, so buy something tasty for yourself, it's been nice, see you around*, as she disappears out the door. But I'm still sitting on top of her stomach. I have something I need to say. Today, I can't just send her on her way. Annoyed, she wriggles and bucks her hips.

—What do you think you're doing? I've got to go.

My thighs choke her little by little.

—Ouch, that hurts! Hey!

—Let's break up.

—Ah.

—It's no fun anymore. You think so too.

—Ah ah ah.

She seems a little flustered but continues.

—Thanks for saying it first. I've had a good time . . .

As I expected, she coolly accepted my suggestion that we end our relationship. However, it doesn't really matter if she accepts it or not. I just wanted to maintain the respect between us as a reward for her devotion.

—I've got something to tell you.

—What is it? Tell me.

Her nostrils palpitate, and she seems to be expecting affectionate reminiscences about the pleasure I've obtained during our time together to spill from my lips like a candy necklace.

—Your breath stinks.

—Huh?

—It makes me want to hurl.

—What?

My mouth blossoms like a flower. Aiming for her head, I chomp down, but all that fills my mouth is a fistful of sweaty hair and a wad of cotton. How dare she deflect my knife when she's on my plate! It's not that surprising since I risked hunting after arousal has died down and our minds have cleared. But my pride is horribly wounded, so the strength I used to hold down her arms and torso accidentally lets up. I've made a stupid mistake, like a rookie who's overturned their plate after screwing up the first cut of their knife. Thanks to this error, the time I'd set aside for the kill has now extended indefinitely. When will I be able to cut her throat? In an hour? In two? I do have other appointments, you know. . . . What'll happen if I can't get her in my hands before the trains stop? That being said, there's no need to worry so much about it right now. As soon as I get ahold of my emotions, I block the exits. She had quickly rolled onto the floor but couldn't do much more. Lying flat on her stomach, she stays as still as the dead. It kind of looks like she's sniffing the floor. I bet she's petrified, too scared to stand up. If she thinks she's going to get the happy ending given to the star of a movie who survives an encounter with man-eating aliens, she'd be wise to give up on that hope sooner than later. For my own replenishment, I must catch her.

She jumps up with a desperate howl and grabs the disposable razor from the counter. Ah, shit, that gave me a fright! She won't be able to cut through more than 0.1 millimeters of my skin with that razor, but her courage in the face of the impossible is admirable. It's been such a long time since I've faced off against such a lively opponent. I decide to observe for a bit, to be better able to predict her movements. Her eyelids are drooping and she's babbling incoherently—it seems like she's asking what I am—and when she waves the razor over her head, I feel a confusing jolt in my heart. It's the first time I've experienced a situation like this, so I'm a teensy bit scared myself. I've gotten caught up in these pathetic feelings not only because she has transformed into a completely different person, but also because I am wondering, does she really want to live that badly? A truth that I had long buried deep in my heart resurfaces: humans have survival instincts and can feel pain. Of course, I am generally aware of that. I've watched humans swallow down their suffering as they are nearly crushed to death on the subway, all in the name of earning money to survive. But for so long, I dispatched them so quickly that the humans never had a chance to feel physical or mental pain, and they certainly had no time to resist. I didn't realize that a human could put up such a fight when confronted with a hunter trying to take their life. I'm frozen with doubt. Can I really kill a human fighting for their life? Is it really okay for me to take that living creature, who is running barefoot and naked trying to get away from me, throwing the television, knocking over the chest of drawers, shattering mirrors, and brandishing clothes hangers, and break them down to fill my refrigerator? Am I not committing a most heinous act that I'll never be able to wash clean of?

My mind may be muddled, but I decide to take the simplest course of action. I chase her with heavy, booming steps, trying to melt her head. Thanks to her quickly changing directions as she tries to get away, the soft soles of my feet slip and my shoulder crashes into the wall. Thank you. I swallow my rage as my toenail claws and strikes the air. Her body is covered in scratches and leaking blood like she is a piece of fruit with patches of its skin peeled back. As I said before, as long as my prey is contained in a room, using tools with exquisite timing, resisting with all its might, it's not easy to cut its throat. Human hide isn't tough like leather, nor is it protected by a shell, so it would all be over if I hooked my toenail on the soft skin on the front of her neck and moved quickly from left to right, but I am piteously flustered. Her death is an utter mess. She brought it upon herself. Her voice is giving out, making it harder to scream. The sad sound of blasts of wind rushing through a narrow opening is all that can be heard, so wretched that it fucking kills me! I'm losing strength bit by bit. My hunger grows accordingly. My desire to devour her straightens me up. In the end, it's a question of time. It's not long till her strength will bottom out. And I am not the me pretending to be human. My body is a horse freed from its reins, a fish ripping through a net, an oriole let out of its cage.

Having tired herself out, she collapses to the ground. Slowly, she slides her ass across the floor, hitting her head against the wall with the window. Now that she is backed into a corner, I think my time has come and, slobbering, make my swift attack. I say swift, but I'm not all that quick. I weigh so much in this body (around 340 kilos) that I can't really run. It takes a bit of time for me to get up to speed. It would be wrong to say I'd be nimble as a rabbit at speed, but the destructive force of my body is nothing to laugh at. She has left me hungry for a long time. I'm apoplectic. When I catch her, I'm not going to leave a single hair behind. Suddenly, she jumps up from being a corpse sprawled on the floor and opens the window with a bang. A chilly night breeze slaps me across the face. Seeing the height of the building, she hesitates, her face crying and in distress, then, looking back and seeing me getting closer by the second, she climbs into the window and hangs on to the frame. She jumps. I only stop myself after I shatter the window.

I look down into the alley. She is lying on the black asphalt, blanketed in glass fragments from the broken windowpane, wailing, *Gaaaaaaah, guahhhhhhh*. To think that her ankle would break from falling only from the second floor. . . . Dragging her leg, she gets as far away from the motel entrance as she possibly can. Thankfully there is no one around. But in a matter of seconds, the people who are sensitive to disturbances will come running. And they'll call the police. Curious guests staying in the motel across the street are standing at their windows. I am stuck debating whether I should follow her in my current state or not. I'm about to lose sight of my meal. I need to make a quick decision. I want to catch her before anyone can offer a hand. I decide that, somehow, I'll be able to hide my transitional half-human-half-monster state in the darkness of the alleyway. No, before I can even make that decision my feet pull me up into the window frame. I'm so hungry! I want to get my wet lips around fresh human meat right this minute! I put on my backpack and jump, floating down like a jellyfish.

Sunlight never reaches this ocean. In this place, no life-form walking with two feet on dry ground, let alone one that has a fucked-up leg and is rocking like a rotten berry, could ever get around quickly or have any hope of avoiding danger. I call out to the one who threw herself into the water, *Comebackpleaseiwon'teatyouIwon'tkillyoureally-Iwon'tIpromiseyoumusthavebeensurprisedI'msorryIsaidI'msorry-rycometomeIloveyouIloveyou*, as I hop along after her. I catch sight of her face, crumpled like an aluminum can, whenever she glances back under a streetlamp. It looks as if another monster has already torn into her. She looks around her and cries in a thin, trembling voice, *Help me! Save me!*

Her voice is incapable of piercing the thick wall of water to ring out. If she opens her mouth, it fills with water, making it harder to get the words out. No one comes to her rescue. They can't help. Any humans who interfere with my hunt will die by my hand. Keep that in mind. She manages to dodge me at every turn in this winding alley as if she has figured out changing direction is my weakness. The sneaky little rat! There's no way she's gotten around me and back into the building or is hiding in the parking garage, is there? Hoo hoo, just you try! Hiding is useless. Like a shark hunting its prey with its nose, all I have to do is follow the long scent trail she leaves behind her. Idly swaying seaweed. Boulders near transparent glass. It'll be more advantageous if she stays out in the open. It'll give her a little more space to dodge my attacks and extend her life.

Anyway, the sooner she understands the situation she's in, the better. I'd like to not prolong her pain. Since meeting me, the only way to end her pain is by accepting death. I'll do it in one blow so it won't hurt. Bloody footprints are stamped clearly on the street. That'll be the fault of the skin scrapping off of the bottoms of her feet. It's tearing my heart apart. She still hasn't given up hope. She's thinking, *I want to eat a hot meal and go to sleep watching a relaxing movie. If only I could feel the light of tomorrow's sun.* . . . I'm sorry to keep repeating myself, but I have no

intention of stopping my hunt. I give her one last chance to end her life of her own volition.

IsaidI'mnotgoingtoeatyousostoprighttherewhycan'tyoutrustmeI'mnotgoingtokillyouIswearpleasecomebacktomeIloveyou! She keeps going forward and doesn't look back. What does she believe that makes her act this way? There aren't any of your kind here, you're all alone. It's been a long time since your planet got blown up. I don't want her pain. Who gets off on seeing people suffer? I can't leave her to move as she pleases. My teeth keep missing the mark, so even if I manage to bite off a chunk of her, I won't be able to hit a vital point. I don't like to overestimate my hunting skills. Biting while running is an unfamiliar move in my hunting style. Before crash landing here, I never needed to hunt. I only had to face off against the meat already on my plate.

I've run out of patience. Playtime is over. I decide to throw myself over her like a net. Keeping an eye on her, I crouch, ready to pounce. As I fly through the air, in an instant, I calculate her trajectory and adjust my own, drawing an arc like a cannonball. I hope that, at the end of the flight path, there is a glossy head. I open my mouth in four parts and lay my teeth flat against my gums. My lips flap wildly. The space inside my cheeks expands to three times the size of my prey. I have made her coffin. *IpromiseIwon'teatyou!* Before she makes it out of the alley and into the road, *Iwon'teatyouIpromise!* my lips embrace her. *Ipromiselwon'teatyou!* As if a blanket fell from the sky, *Iwon'teatyouIpromise!* she tries her hardest to survive, *IpromiseIwon'teatyou!* punching the inside of my mouth. With a shhhhhhhhhhhhh I expel the air *Iwon'teatyouIpromise!* and press my mucous membrane *IpromiseIwon'teatyou!* to her skin. I drag my extended mouth down *Iwon'teatyouIpromise!* the inky blackness of a different alley *IpromiseIwon'teatyou!* and crush her to a pulp. My saliva pumps more *Iwon'teatyouIpromise!* actively than ever, *IpromiseIwon'teatyou!* melting her. Her flesh and bones become a coagulated rice-porridge-like mush, *Iwon'teatyouIpromise!* then slide down *IpromiseIwon'teatyou!* my throat. Finally, *Iwon'teatyouIpromise!* I've eaten *Ipromiselwon'teatyou!* every last *Iwon'teatyouIpromise!* bit of her.

Except the hair.

I don't feel like going home early tonight. My heart is all mixed up, so even if I were to clean myself up and lie down in bed, sleep would never come. Now that my rowdy appetite has been put to rest, my mind clears as if I am wiping crud from my eyes. It's now possible to ruminate and meditate in a peaceful atmosphere. I throw up a chunk of flesh from the top half of her body onto a telephone pole. This is the first time I've thrown up human meat. I'm in shock. It feels like I've eaten something I shouldn't have. I really didn't know. I never fully understood. No, I clearly knew once, but as time passed, I cut off any routes to that kind of perception. Really, I've never forgotten. The persistent grind of meat.

This is a story from before I butchered on white blankets without spilling a drop of blood. Back then, the walls were dripping in blood-soaked organ chunks, a sight so gruesome that it's difficult to put into words. I used to go around eating meat without a thought, and the meat would gush blood and die slow, painful deaths. Without exception, if their legs were severed, they'd pull themselves with their arms, and if their arms were cut off too, they would inch themselves like a caterpillar. Screaming! Screaming! Screaming! Screaming like they were a life-form specifically born to do it. I used all the energy I got from feeding on cleaning and doing laundry. I couldn't help but wonder if it was causing more harm than good when all the calories I spent hunting were replenished by the fresh meat only to be burnt away doing the cleanup.

But I've mastered the trick to energy-efficient hunting: seizing the opportunity right after salacious sex to bite off the head of my one-night stand and suck out their blood. This is the hunting method that I would recommend to any being like myself living on Earth. Without fail, this is how you must do it, dear reader. Humans are so easily made into meat, without any pangs of conscience. And if you are struck by a bout of conscience, never fear! For conscience quickly crumbles with repeated evil deeds. Time solves all. An unpredictable murder with seemingly no time to feel pain conceals the incontrovertible fact that the victim fears death, that they are an animal whose life is powered by that fear. It reduces the meaning of death. By eliminating the wretched screams from death, the line between human and object blurs. As long as I am certain that they can't feel their deaths bodily, I can pop as many as I like into my belly and digest them. My burden decreases when I highlight the differences between me and them. If they were the same as me, I couldn't eat them. And even if they were like me, if I were to believe that I am fundamentally on a different level, I could devour them without a second thought. The moment that belief breaks . . . I have trouble eating, or I throw up. I'm thinking of them: my meals, the humans I owe my life to, the life-forms typically made with two arms and two legs, the beings that are capable of throwing themselves out of windows in order to live.

This is the rooftop of a five-story building. A spring breeze swirls past. My hair joins in the swell. The heavens are scattered with as many stars as humans that I have chewed up and swallowed down. My burps are a pungent mixture of her sweat, blood, and perfume. Don't even mention the farts. No matter how you look at it, my life is fucked up. I kill humans before their time is up, fill my belly, spit up what I barely managed to eat, and look up at the night sky to gaze at the stars, hahaha. I've lost my appetite, but when tomorrow morning comes, with no trouble at all, I'll fry up the meat I have marinating and savor every bite, all the while doing my best to forget what happened today. Right now, there's no way that I could eat human flesh, and I think I'll have a hard time handling human meat forever after. But tomorrow, tomorrow will be different. I will remember today as a day I worked myself so hard my bones nearly fell out. A sigh pushes open my jaw and escapes my mouth. A truly tiring day. If I'm going to tackle tomorrow's schedule, I better get some rest. It's not long till the last train. I'll see you again in fourteen hours. Goodnight, sleep tight.

Have you eaten breakfast? How about lunch? I'm sitting at the table dipping sashimi in a sauce of gochujang and vinegar. The texture is so springy and cold that it makes my mouth tingle as I savor each bite. At first, I speared each piece on my toenail before placing it in my mouth, but I became greedy and now shove my nose to the plate, swallowing fistfuls of meat. As soon as the plate is empty, I am full of remorse and lick up the lemon juice remaining on the surface. I skip over washing the dishes and slink to the bathroom to brush my teeth. Looking at the reflection in the mirror, I try puffing up my always-cool bone shield. The twenty-six horns, each with their own length and diameter, fan out like a peacock's tail feathers. Unfortunately, there is no life-form here that can appreciate the seductive powers of a prospective partner's decorative headpiece. And on top of that, it saddens me that there is no one here that would give the spots clearly marked on my body the respect they deserve. I can't compliment myself. Immediately, my feelings for my face in the mirror turn to hate. A face that's useless, good for nothing. Thanks to the beauty standards on this planet, I've become much uglier than I was before. Hideous. Ugly people (although I'm not a person) deserve to die. Or at least cover their faces. People who are confident in spite of their ugliness are the ugliest. I've learned that my face arouses homicidal impulses. That there'd be nothing said if I were stoned to death in the street. That no one will be sad when I die. I focus on picking out the limp bits of food stuck between my teeth. My mood may be down in the dumps, but in the hour and a half or so that I take to pick my teeth, I forget my sorry state. And then I have an afternoon wank or two.

My no-longer-heavy body leaves the bathroom and opens the windows to freshen the air. The weather is bright and sunny, so my morning schedule wraps up nicely without a hitch. Moving on, I have an evening appointment waiting for me at a quarter past six. Enjoying the refreshing breeze, I sit in

the pilot's seat, l o o k i n g   t h r o u g h   t h e   m e s -
s a g e s   t h a t   c a m e   i n   o v e r n i g h t . Before that,
I removed the people I have dealt with from my f a -
v o r i t e s   ♥   l i s t and erase our chat history. If you
don't delete your records from time to time, you'll be able
to know at a glance the date and frequency of eating out. I
don't want to think about my diet. K i l l   a n d   e a t .
That's it. Who would want to remember the s p e e c h patterns, the p h y s i q u e , and more of the p r e d e a t h ap-
p e a r a n c e of meat in their refrigerator? After I straighten
up what's on the screen, I make plans for a   n e w   m e a l .

hOtBttm: We're meeting tomorrow, right?

Hunt1ng4love: Yes, that's right.

hOtBttm: Can I see some more pictures?

Hunt1ng4love: Sure.

hOtBttm: You're just my type.

Hunt1ng4love: Thank you. Send me one too.

hOtBttm: I'm ugly, aren't I?

Hunt1ng4love: Not at all. You look good.

hOtBttm: Ah, I wanna fuck right now.

Hunt1ng4love: Me too.

hOtBttm: What's your voice sound like?

Hunt1ng4love: Very deep. You?

hOtBttm: It's not high. Pretty average.

Hunt1ng4love: I'm kinda busy right now. I'll message you later.

hOtBttm: Ah, of course you are. I'm not bothering you, am I?
Hunt1ng4love: You're a nuisance, idiot.

I don't have time to be wasting on repeating the same tedious conversation we had
before. I only have conversations essential
to meeting up with the people I've made
dates with.

Obviously, I don't hit send. I close the chat window and mess with some other humans. I've got to
ask at least one other person. Because I
don't want to have conversations. No, sometimes
I enjoy having conversations with people that I
connect with but have never met in person (and
who don't look that tasty). Although usually, it doesn't
last more than a day before I cut contact.
Sometimes they start to feel like an old friend. As long
as we keep talking, it feels like I have a friend.
The type of friend that you can call up whenever to
have a meal. A friend to chat with in a bar who'd say,
Let's go to karaoke, and drag me along. A friend
that I've spent so much time with that there is a chance
we may become lovers. I find a friend like that once
every couple of months, but they disappear before
the day is through. I confess to them all the

w o r r i e s that I normally don't speak of, and they do the same with me. Sharing my worries with myself is impossible. I already know my w o r r i e s . I'm not hoping for solutions. I n e e d s o m e o n e w h o w i l l l i s t e n .   No, I'm asking for a person who will steal away my time with good conversation. I'm so busy I could die, but I'm also not the least bit busy, with a l l t h e t i m e i n t h e w o r l d on my hands. Sometimes I have so much time it sickens me. Please take up my time! Not my body, but my time, time together with me. S t e a l a s m u c h a s y o u l i k e . Just a moment is fine too. It's better if we meet in person. A n d even better than that if you don't get creeped out by my true form and back away. P l e a s e give me attention, p l e a s e give me some love. A h , I ' m a s k i n g f o r t o o m u c h , forgive me (a formality). But if I were to try and make friends, is there any other way than to s p l i t m y s e l f i n t w o ? But the other half of me is s t i l l me, so what's the use in that? Sorry, forgive me! I ' l l s t o p . I've got to shut down the screens if I'm going to m a k e i t t o t h e r h i - n o c e r o s ' s p l a c e by six fifteen.

Now, I'll go back to being a w o m a n . Because what they want is a w o m a n . No other reason. I p r e p a r e t o t r a n s f o r m m y s e l f in front of the mirror. Following the manual, the one I've cobbled together on my own

these long years, I start with w i d e   h i p s , a slender
waist, narrow shoulders, and a v o l u p t u o u s chest.
I use b e a r d h a i r , l e g h a i r , and a r m p i t h a i r to
l e n g t h e n the hair on my head. What I c r a f t b e -
t w e e n m y t w o l e g s is not a cock and pair of balls,
nor it is a set of balls and a pussy, nor is it a pussy with a
cock, just a s i n g l e p i n k p u s s y . Things get a bit d i c e y
when you mix all three. It's a problem if it's t o o b i g or
too small, or if the depth is t o o d e e p or too shallow. Whatever it is, w h a t ' s a p p r o p r i a t e i s
b e s t . I'm not really sure what exactly makes something
appropriate, b u t i t ' s g o t t o b e a p p r o -
p r i a t e . For the finale, I d e c k m y f a c e o u t with a
set of w e l l - d e f i n e d e y e s , n o s e , a n d l i p s and a
slim jaw. Finished! Like solving a Rubik's cube.

But before I step onto the stage, I have something left
to prepare. Before the cameras are operating, an actor
must become their character, and they must wear the cos-
tume that fits the character. I'll be playing the part of a
woman in her late twenties. Acting as a woman is far more
intricate than acting as a man. Men can walk however
they like, but a woman must walk like a woman. "However they like" means walking with their legs splayed and
their shoulders shaking. "Like a woman" means turning
your knees inward and jiggling your ass. I don't need to
spell it out for you. . . . Those who know, know and execute

it with their bodies. They put effort into the execution. They will often fail. They'll be scared of failure. They'll give up too. It's actually hard to tell walking styles apart by gender. Because it's all in your head. That's why, when I was first learning to walk like a human, I couldn't, for the life of me, figure out the difference between men and women. In my eyes, all humans looked exactly the same. I thought that things that look alike move alike. To put it a different way, I wondered how it was even possible to divide something with so many visible variants into just two groups. But humans keep bringing up their criteria and judge me by it. In the subway, in the street, in restaurants, in shopping malls, in parks . . . their expressions and words that question my humanity irrespective of where I am made me tear myself apart and rebuild myself piece by piece. I've invested close to ten years of my time figuring out what exactly their criteria are. My conclusion is that there are no such criteria. So, I just learned how to act as if there were. How shall I put it? I've figured out how to read mainstream body trends. Two trends with blurred and fluid boundaries. I've picked up how to pretend they can be explained when they are inexplicable. Criteria are like glass. As long as they are respected and held without dropping them, they'll stay solid and won't break. I made myself complicit in humanity's scam and adapted myself to the local ecosystem. That being said, I still don't feel an intimate sense of belonging, but at least I don't starve.

Since we're already talking about this bullshit, why don't I go on? When you want to be a woman, follow my advice. Speak in a thin, pretty voice. It has to be high-pitched. Try pushing it up into your nose. Cover your mouth when you laugh. Press down firmly and neatly when writing. Grow your hair to your shoulders. Curls are discouraged. Flap your wrists often. Show enthusiasm about grocery shopping and cooking. Beef up your cooking skills. Be unfailingly kind to others—especially men. Use your charm to get out of danger. Fall in love with a man. Eat very little. Even if you really want to finish it, leave some on your plate. Make sure you attain a slim figure and maintain it for your whole life. Play dumb, with no regard for your actual intelligence. Disparage your driving. Be chatty. Try your best to sincerely enjoy cleaning and doing laundry. Think of weakness as a virtue, and let your strength rot away. Wear makeup even in your dreams. Wear bright clothing. Conceal your sexual appetite, and take it to your grave. Become shyness incarnate. . . . There's a fuckton more where that all comes from. I just couldn't write it all down. To act the part of a woman, you've got to memorize a hefty script. Men should do the opposite. Just don't act like a woman.

Ah, but it is terribly difficult to memorize the whole script. Just because I've memorized it doesn't mean I can stick it to my body like another leg. I've learned the trick to pretending I've put my heart and soul into memorizing. Anyone can slip out of the criteria. People are nice enough to close their eyes and look away when you make a mistake. Mistakes can only be tolerated so much, so you've got to understand where the boundary for what's intolerable lies. If you're going to make mistakes, make them well. That is the crux of the matter. Do you think I should write a textbook for all the newbies freshly landed on Earth who don't know what's what? There's no reason for the humans I encounter in my hunting radius to represent all of humanity, or all the life-forms on this planet, but any aliens who are chased off their home planet without warning and try to sneak onto this planet as a refugee should come see me. I've got it aaaAaaall ready. Since the feast is already prepared, all you need to bring is yourselves. I'll gladly spoon-feed you. Just come, please.

I am a womanly woman wearing a blouse, skirt, and heels. As a womanly woman, I carefully climb the iron staircase I've built to practice on. My womanly woman ass cheeks bob up and down like a buoy floating in the ocean. Even I think I look elegant. I should be holding a basket and scattering flower petals in front of me as I walk back down the stairs. I look tranquil on the outside, but thanks to the unfriendly height and surface area of my heels, it feels like I'm about to twist my ankle and fall down the stairs, making an unsightly mess of myself. I've lost a chance to add more femininity. I'll try again next time. It's wrong of me to demand my body do things even humans find hard. Please forgive me, my body. I've put on some low-heeled sandals for you. Now that I've slung my bag across my shoulders to finish my disguise, I am camera ready. When I leave the house, unseen cameras will start shooting me. I've got to get my head on straight.

It's around five o'clock in the evening. The sunlight is melting and dripping from the branches like raindrops. It flashes across the metallic shell of my home, like the scales of a dragon flying into the sun. I live all alone in this beautiful, spacious home. Sometimes the world that I'm wrapped up in feels needlessly rich. The life of luxury passes me by. Like how the fertility of the forest floor and the lushness of the trees is wholly unrelated to my position. In this world there are traps set up to ensnare strangers, like somehow tripping and falling into a hole. Looking up at the world from 10 m below everyone else. They all look down on me, trapped in a sinkhole. They don't even have a reason to make the time to look down on me. They've got everything, the wild plains, rivers, oceans, and skies, and cities constructed to match the way their bodies are built. They are sucking on the teat of infrastructure they were born for. All around me is darkness that I fear to touch.

I can only see something if I make the great effort to lift my head to look in the direction of the light. A corner of my house enters my field of vision. This house truly is a habitat just for me. But I feel like I'm viewing a stranger's house from far away in a cave that, unbeknownst to me, is slowly collapsing. There are dark shadows cast in my house. The world as I perceive it is mostly shrouded in darkness. Do I exist in the same physical space as other people? Can I really seek joy and pleasure together with them? Why does the path become narrower the further I walk down it? Why is every place I go to a cliff? Self-pity pins me down like a boulder, and I struggle with it until

I arrive at the subway station.

Yes,

yet

again

again

again

again

again I am taking the train. Taking swerving steps, I must get back into the cycle. Somehow, the process of taking the elevator, tapping my card, getting on the train, and finding a seat goes smoothly. I set my bag on top of my thighs and take a look around. There are cameras here and cameras over there as well. There are old cameras and new cameras. Cameras to carry with you. Standing cam-

eras, sitting cameras, cameras riding wheelchairs, yawn-
ing cameras, dozing cameras, sleeping cameras, chatting
cameras, cracking-up cameras, angry cameras, passionate
gaming cameras, music-listening cameras, begging cameras, ignoring cameras, swearing cameras . . . and even a
camera on my insides filming me. The cameras don't know
who they are. When one camera shoots another, they too
are shot. Cameras that are shot and are shooting each
other. Surveilling and being surveilled. Being surveilled
and surveilling. I cast off any delusions with a shake of my
head. I've got to get to sleep. Sleep, dear reader, is restor-
ative. I'mgettingsleepygettingsleepygettingsleepygetting-
sleepygettingsleepy . . .

   If sometime, somewhere, I could forget—if only for a
second—that cameras are following me, then I could close
the gap between myself and the part I am playing. It might
just disappear. You, dear reader, earnestly play all your parts.
The roles that were assigned to you without your consent
are stuck to your body like a label: A label that you can't re-
move before death. A label that can't be removed even after death. The labels are invisible. They're not really there,
you know. They've melted into your flesh. They may have
even made their home in a deeper, more abstract part of
you. You won't be able to fish them out even if you're sliced
up to the point that your bones are exposed and your guts
are spilling out of your carcass. Really does your head in,

doesn't it? Imagine someone has, without your knowledge, stuck an expletive-filled sticker on your back. The sticker absorbs the looks from other people and, before you know it, grows large enough to cover your skin with no signs of stopping. It tries to control your identity. I don't think you understand the true nature of the sticker, dear reader. It's okay if you don't. You've got to not know to be fine. I've consciously tried my damnedest to receive a sticker. And I'll have to keep it up. I am always conscious of my acting. To become one with your sticker—this is near impossible for me. A mole that naturally shows up on your face and a mole that you draw where you want it may be inherently different, but when the two can't be told apart by the naked eye they become the same. I survive by tricking the eye. What's all this nonsense, you say? Just think of it as the ramblings of a life-form pretending to be human. It won't be that important to you, dear reader.

I am slowly sinking into the lazy waters of a river. I'm about to give myself fully to sleep, which sucks me in without noticing its touch because it is the same temperature as my body, when the person sitting next to me strokes my thigh. Breathing in the body odor, I'd say it's an old man in his fifties or sixties. He probably wants to slip his hand under my skirt and touch my cock, no, my pussy. The kind of bastard who'd stay even after he pulls down my panties and penetrate me with his fingers. I catch his arm.

I make a hole in the palm of my hand and unsheathe my toenail. As fast as a wasp stings, I rapidly stab his wrist, cutting off the hand. To keep from getting blood on me, I push him toward the aisle. Passengers scatter like startled birds. Police and paramedics will be arriving soon. They won't suspect me. How could a girl with a pretty face and a banging body hurt someone without a deadly weapon? Inconceivable! What a shame. He won't touch a pussy again, he's so scared. Why don't you jerk off with your stump, hahahahaha! I'm infinitely grateful to the cute old man rolling around screaming on the floor. He has proven the excellence of my acting. I'm a real woman!

He's a real fucking dog. Ah, forgive me. I've accidentally lumped dogs in with the likes of him. I would like to give a sincere apology to all the dogs of Earth. I can almost hear their complaints now. Bow wow! Woof woof! Bark as much as you like. Fight back against the humans who have used your good name as a curse. I resemble a dog. I'm closer to a dog than a human, although humans eat dogs and I eat humans, but that's beside the point. I also exist as a curse passing from one human mouth to another. My heart goes out to the dogs. It'd be nice to bring one home with me. I'd make it meals of minced up human organs. The dog would wag its tail in excitement. Why have I never thought of this before? A dog might even become my best friend. Although I don't know what the dog's opinion might be. No, what am I hoping for here? What would be different with a dog? Obviously, a dog couldn't handle my disgusting face. It'll only lick me and wag its tail when I fix myself up like a human, won't it? I'm a little closet crammed full of everything that was strewn across the living room and bedroom floors when you get the sudden news that a guest is coming over. The poor little closet that doesn't know when its contents might burst out while the guest is present. A dog would get riled up, running around and drooling, and inevitably bump into the closet. Do you know what I mean? BOOM! The closet explodes. All of my tightly locked away secrets come flying out of the closet toward the dog's head. Will the dog be able to bear the weight of my secrets? It'll run out of the house like its tail is on fire.

Dammit, I got lost in my thoughts and ended up here because of that old fart. I'm sorry. I can't block the countless branches from sprawling. Maybe that's why I'm always hungry. Hearing rumbling coming from my stomach, I long to see the rhinoceros. I think the old man has gone to reattach his hand. I promptly take advantage of the mass of passengers rushing off the train. I take a good long look at the signs hanging from the ceiling, and after checking my surroundings a few times, I keep aware of where the bumpy yellow tiles are on the floor so as not to trip as I cautiously walk away. The train screeches as it accelerates and leaves the station. I stare into the empty tunnel that sucked up the train

until I reach the start of the stairs. I wonder how many people that rickety old train has had aboard it in its lifetime, and how many people it has crushed. I don't think I'll ever figure out the answer, but I lock myself into these kinds of pointless thoughts in order to lessen, even just a little bit, the burden of climbing the stairs. I'm distracting myself. When I extract myself from these trains of thought I often find myself at the top of the stairs. Today, however, I have a bad feeling that the pain in my legs will be eating away at me. Someone once said that all that's left for a person who's fallen down to do is to climb back up again, and, yes, what they said is true. What I must climb up is the stairs. There are still twenty steps left. I stop on the fourth step to catch my breath. Am I in poor condition today? Sometimes I've got to go up and down stairs to find out. The stairs gauge my condition. And according to today's reading, I'm beaten to a pulp. Thanks for letting me know, stairs. Being a mess is totally different from knowing you're a mess. A pessimistic mood always comes to the surface of my mind and body when I least want it—like when I'm mounting a steep staircase—and beats me over the head. It's pouring gas and fanning the flames of a house fire. (Is this the right situation for this idiom?) How can it hold up without wavering? Am I made of steel?

I hear the voice of an angel.

—Can I help you with your bag?

—No, it's fine, haha.

I say that out of habit; I fucking hate it when a stranger puts their hands on my bag. Just as it is wrong to grab my pussy, it's wrong to grab my bag. I'll kill you.

—Aren't you tired?

—I'm not.

My knees feel like they'll split into eight pieces, but I grit my teeth.

—It looks really heavy though.

Does he have shit blocking up his ears? It looks like he has no intention of leaving me be. It's ticking me off. I am trying my hardest to look perfectly fine with each step. The angel was watching me nervously, afraid that I might fall. Imagining beating the crap out of him with my bag— *I'd be fine if only you'd fuck off!*—keeps me going.

—Don't be like this, give it to me, quickly.

The incomparable angel puts words in my mouth.

—It's my bag.

—Huh?

—I said it's mine!

—Aren't you a piece of work.

The bastard doesn't go on his way; instead, smiling innocently, he makes to grab the straps of my bag without permission. But even if all my fingers fall off my hands, he

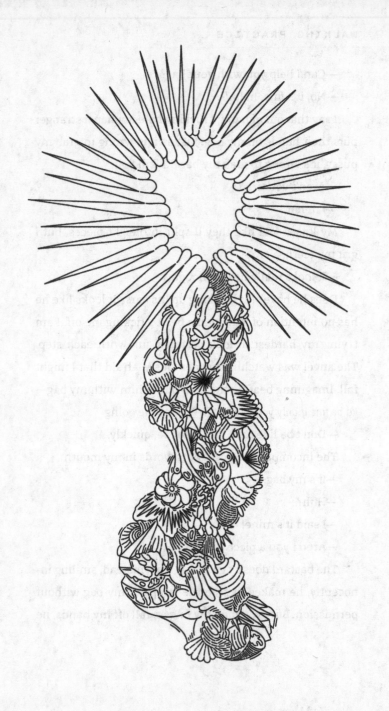

will never take this bag from me. This bag is an extension of my body. I can't leave it to anyone else.

—It's mine! It's my bag! Mine!

There seemed to be no end to the scuffle in sight. The people rushing up and down the stairs keep sneaking glances but don't interfere. As always, no human will come to my aid. Why won't they help me? Would they help if I shouted for help? I'm scared to ask for help, since it's likely that my cries for help will go unanswered. I'm afraid I'll once again confirm that I am completely alone. Then what remains of my now shameful, miserable skull might just explode with a POP!

Ah ah, if only I was a little less disgusting. . . .

AAAAAAAAAAAAAAAAAAAAAHHHHHHHHHHHHHHHH

The bastard doesn't pay any mind to their stares and confidently persists with the bag. It frustrates me to no end that I don't have enough strength to slice him with my toenail. *Tenacious fucker! Tiresome shithead! Piss off! Fucking die! Why the fuck are you doing this to me?* I strip the fucker's clothes off. He's tied up with rope and hanging upside-down from the ceiling. I take one of his testicles, *probably* stuck, trembling, to his smelly crotch, into my mouth and bite down till it bursts. Then I pierce his belly with my hand. Pushing past the fat layer and his maze of intestines, hooking my toenail around his vertebrae, I snap out his spine piece by piece. It takes eighteen fucking minutes and twenty-eight fucking seconds.

—At least give me your number.

This is what the bastard has to say when he finally lets go of my bag. Number, number, number!!! So getting my number was the goal, the jerk! How fucking cute! I smile as if throwing up in my mouth. I had to suffer this fool just because he wanted my number!

—No, you fucking loser.

The bastard's face chills and stiffens like a hunk of meat shoved in the darkest corner of my freezer. I wouldn't be surprised if he grabbed me by my hair and threw me down the stairs. But still, he's handsome as a motherfucker. So handsome I want to give him my bag, my body, my everything. Light is beaming from his face. His ass and thighs look as solid as watermelons heavy with juice, and his cock is probably substantial—a plentiful plate of sashimi—enough not to disappoint me. He's got every elite physical quality that would get me to send tens of messages if I found him on an app. Should I have sweetly given him my number instead of losing my temper? It might have been nice, after all this time, to play at dating a human then eat them up in a motel. But he's already buzzed off. All that's left are the lovely stairs and me. I hope that bastard comes to me in my dreams tonight. It'd be nice to pack him into

my airtight containers to put in my bag after he licks my
ear and says he loves me.

As I support myself on the leisurely moving walkway,
I try my hardest to scrub the mouthwatering afterimage
of his hindquarters from my mind. Even if I am licking out
his sopping asshole in my dreams, first, I must give my
fullest attention to the rhinoceros. I've got to make them
feel like they're all I've got in this life. That's how I'll get
the most pleasure and finish without mistakes. I'm inter-
rupted by a text.

—Sorry, could we meet up another time?

It's like the world is trying to kill me.

—I'm already on my way. I'm almost there.

I'm not ready to die yet.

—Where are you?
—In front of your place.
—Huh? I don't see you.
—Just kidding, I have one stop left.
—Ah, I see . . .
—Why, what's wrong?

—I'm just not feeling well, that's all.

—I'm not feeling well either.

—Ah . . . then I'll wait.

—If you didn't want to do it, you should have said so earlier.

—No, it's fine.

Is this some kind of plot? I don't want to meet up with a human who's seeing me begrudgingly. Hookups can only be accomplished if both parties are willing. If I'm going to be rubbing my body up on someone else's, I've got to get their consent. But from the perspective of the one who takes the time and effort to enter foreign lands, if I can't get any meat, that would be a tremendous loss. Promises are precious. You can't just break promises whenever you like. If they have even one drop of conscience left, they won't ghost me. I hope that I have the right address.

I'm cooling off and catching my breath in front of the apartment building. Since the journey from the forest to their house was so arduous, I almost give in to my impulses and lie down in the middle of the road for a five-ton truck to run me over. There were no seats on the train I transferred onto, the escalator was broken, and to top it off, their place was around 1.6 km from the subway exit up a steep inclined road that isn't even marked on the map. Gravity oppresses me with the indifference of a cloud. I'm already shoved into a hole, so how much deeper does it want to push me? The warm spring sunshine is strangling me. It seems that depression and lethargy have nothing to do with the weather. My condition can be ruined when it rains, because it rains, and when the skies are clear, because they're clear. The weather is the weather. The weather isn't doing anything wrong. The weather doesn't concern itself with the likes of me. Where could the key to unraveling my tangled mind and body be? And what form might it take? Nothing will change if I curse the mother-fuckers who crane their necks hoping to see me disappear either by my own hand or another's. Try as I might (in my heart) to murder them, it's no use. . . . That fact haunts me.

I'm off to meet them. The glacier-like stairs await me. Luckily, there are only five steps. On the manageable side. Apartment 101 is right in front of me. Living on a lower floor is enough of a reason for me to consider taking the rhinoceros on as a new partner. And in the case that they are also good with their tongue, they'll fit right in as my eleventh partner—if I disregard the facts that they used being sick as an excuse to treat me like trash, I had a hor-rible journey, and the building is at the top of a hill, that is.

I am holding tight to the handrail on the stairs as if I were a rock climber hanging from a rope. Urgh urgh urgh urgh urgh urgh urgh urgh urgh urgh urgh urgh urgh urgh urgh. I'm sorry for describing climbing stairs so pain-fully every time. (What do you want? It's painful!) Don't start hating stairs on my account. Don't hate me. They say that taking the stairs instead of the elevator is healthier for you and saves electricity, dear reader. Yahoo! I've made it to the top. I've reached the summit. Taking no time to celebrate, I knock on the door to 101.   Knock knock.

Knock   knock. Knock   knock.   Knock   .   .   . knock.   Knock knock. . . .   There's no response. I've made a misstep. I drop to the floor. My legs have puddled under me like a snowman getting rained on at the end of winter. I've lost the will to stand up.

—Come in.

Just as I was thinking of rolling myself down the stairs, the door cracks open and I hear a nasal voice. The rhinoceros has yet to reveal themselves. As if they don't want me to see their face. I hang my fingers on the door handle and restack my legs as if restoring a collapsed tower. They are standing stiffly inside the entryway, waiting for their hookup to let themselves in. Are they steadying their nerves? Or just an introvert? I dither a bit, then quickly snap the door open. As soon as I do, they jump back in surprise. Ah . . . so it wasn't a rhinoceros lumbering in here, but an elephant. I've been conned. This can't be happening. This can't be happening to me. Am I dreaming? How would I transport elephant meat?! It's so heavy I won't even be able to get it into the bathroom. It'll be hard enough to suck all the blood out. They don't weigh 83 kg like they said, more like 130 kg at the lightest. No matter how well they suck my nipples or how tasty the meat is, if I can't cleanly butcher it and take it back home with me, what's the point? I'm here to stock up on rations. And I can't stand dirtying the sheets!

—What are you doing? Come in.

—Ah, yes . . .

—You're prettier in real life.

—Thank you.

—It's been a long time for me . . .

The elephant's face goes red.

—Huh?

—. . . since I've met anyone.

—Ah, is that right?

—I was so nervous and shaking that I thought maybe we could meet up next time.

—Are you telling me to leave?

—Ah, no! No! As soon as I saw you, it's fine.

Spit flying as they wave their hands furiously.

—Let's not beat around the bush and get to it. I'm about to pass out, I'm so tired.

I kick off my shoes and set my bag down in front of the bathroom door. Sucking hard on the elephant's thick tongue, I pull them in the direction of the bed. The apartment is so tiny that we only take three steps before rolling onto the damp, yellowing blankets. This elephant must have been starving for five years, since they use their tusks to rip off my clothes and take me in their mouth. There is no part of my body their tongue does not get to. They dive right in, without excluding any hard-to-reach spots, and carve a tingling sensation into me that won't go away for days. Like the staff that parted the red sea, any and every hole in my body is about to be spread wide open. I've never used an organ hot enough to peel off my flesh, yet so soft. When they rub their penis-like protruding clit—or perhaps their clit-like slender penis—against my pussy, I white out and forget what I came to do. My mind is scrambled. It feels like my head is blasting off into space. Haaah haaah, they break me down to my bones and put me back together again. I've lost. I've completely surrendered. Professions of love flow from my lips. From this day forward they are my partner. No, I want to date them for a long, long time. At this point, I'd even throw a wedding. I want to play around with their tongue every single day!

I hold them close like a lover would under the blankets, scared to think about when they were last washed. Is this real? I feel like I'm being pampered by a cowhide sofa covered in sheepskin cushions. I can't quite tell the smell of their spit from the smell of shit. Every inch of my skin stinks of rotting feces. But what does that matter? Life is still worth living. Dammit, I broke my cardinal rule of biting off my partner's head after they reach orgasm. I'm not even

surprised. The pillowy arms currently wrapped around my shoulders and waist should be rolling around the bathroom floor. But I want to let their arms keep holding me. It's too hard for me to butcher them anyway. If you want to criticize me, go ahead. This person and I are going to get married.

—You have really nice hair . . .

They stroke my head.

—Thank you.

—I love you.

—I love you too.

—Are you comfortable?

—I'm fine.

—Really?

—Really.

—I love you.

—I love you too.

—I love you more.

—No, I love you more.

—Do you wanna sleep over?

—Ah . . .

Now I remember what time my next appointment is at. My mountain of work floods back into my mind like the tides.

—I've got somewhere to be. I've got to go.

As I roll onto my side, I catch sight of the silent door.

—Right now?

—Yeah, right now.

—Stay a little longer. I don't have any plans . . .

Playing it cute, they hug me tight as if to shatter my skeleton. I can't breathe, and my thoughts are paralyzed. I don't have confidence in a counterattack in my exhausted state. Although I came to hunt, I think it was all in vain and I'm the one being hunted. The front door goes hazy.

—L-later . . . I'll call you later.

—Okay.

They must have understood me since my restraints are quickly released. Except for the hand that grabs my wrist as I try to stand up from the bed. Their eyes are so sad and subtly threaten me as if to say I'm going to break your wrist and deglove your hand. I peel their chubby fingers off me one at a time.

I search the clothes that dizzyingly cover the floor like feathers for something wearable. They ripped everything, including my socks and underwear. Sitting hunched over on the bed, they're probably waiting on tenterhooks for me to make my decision. They see me take a change of clothes out of my bag and think, What a pro. A couple of beads of sweat drip down my face as I try to quickly put myself together without rubbing off my makeup. Even though I left the house after having a late lunch, my bag remains completely empty. I'm so hungry my stomach is ready to ache, I want so badly to sink my teeth into the shoulder that is waving their arm. I don't think losing an arm would be much of an obstacle in lovemaking, but before I run and bite an arm off them, I close the door and run out of the building, shoving a fistful of jerky down my gullet.

My fourth appointment

begins.

hOtBttm: What're you doing right now?

Hunt1ng4love: Nothing~

hOtBttm: Have you had lunch?

Hunt1ng4love: Yes.

Hunt1ng4love: How about you?

hOtBttm: I've eaten too.

Hunt1ng4love: Why do you keep messaging me?

hOtBttm: What do you mean?

Hunt1ng4love: We're just hooking up, but you have so many questions.

hOtBttm: Ah, sorry! It's my first time.

Hunt1ng4love: Make sure you're not late.

hOtBttm: Yes, sorry!

Hunt1ng4love: What's up?

hOtBttm: Ah, me? I, um, I'm just lying in bed.

Hunt1ng4love: Is that right?

hOtBttm: Have you had a lot of hookups?

Hunt1ng4love: One or two . . .

hOtBttm: Ahhhh.

Hunt1ng4love: Are you in college?

hOtBttm: Nope, I've got a job. I work the night shift.

Hunt1ng4love: Why are you looking for hookups?

hOtBttm: I'm just . . . lonely. Can't get a boyfriend.

Hunt1ng4love: Have you ever had one?

hOtBttm: Only one. A few years back. Hby?

Hunt1ng4love: I've never had one.

hOtBttm: You seem like you'd be popular tho . . .

Hunt1ng4love: There are some special circumstances.

hOtBttm: Ah, what do you do for work?

Hunt1ng4love: It's a secret.

hOtBttm: Ah, okay.

Hunt1ng4love: Actually . . . I'm an alien.

hOtBttm: Ahahahaha, really?

Hunt1ng4love: It's not a joke.

hOtBttm: Then . . . how'd you get here?

Hunt1ng4love: There was a war. . . . The enemy forces were chasing me, and I crashed on Earth. I think I'm the only one here. I haven't been able to make contact with anyone else. I've run out of fuel, so I can't go home. Well, my home has disappeared anyway. I've been living like this for fifteen years.

hOtBttm: That sucks.

Hunt1ng4love: You think I'm fucking nuts, don't you?

hOtBttm: Ah, not at all!

Hunt1ng4love: Liar! Who'd believe me . . .

hOtBttm: Ummm . . . Can you eat our food?

Hunt1ng4love: Huh? Yeah, the food is okay.

hOtBttm: That's lucky.

Hunt1ng4love: Yup.

hOtBttm: So, you're on your ship right now?

Hunt1ng4love: Yes, it's in a forest.

hOtBttm: Ah, what a nice place to live.

Hunt1ng4love: Want me to give you a tour?

hOtBttm: That'd be great.

Hunt1ng4love: After we meet, if it works out, I'll invite you over.

hOtBttm: Woo, I'm excited.

Hunt1ng4love: You don't sound that excited.

hOtBttm: I'm very excited. Really. Woo woo!

Idiot. I want to fucking kill him.

hOtBttm: But why don't you look like an alien?

Hunt1ng4love: How do you think aliens are supposed to look?

hOtBttm: Well, they look a certain way in the movies.

Hunt1ng4love: And what's that?

hOtBttm: Bluish-gray skin, a big head, eyes as big as fists, and long skinny arms and legs. . . .

Hunt1ng4love: That's not how I look. And I've never seen any species that look like that.

hOtBttm: Is that so? It's all made up?

Hunt1ng4love: Yes.

hOtBttm: I see. Did you perhaps transform into a human?

Hunt1ng4love: Of course. It's the only way I can hook up with humans like you.

hOtBttm: Hahahaha, that makes sense.

Hunt1ng4love: I wouldn't survive if I didn't.

hOtBttm: What do you look like? Originally.

Hunt1ng4love: I have bright yellow lizard skin, red polka dots, blue fur, three legs, one arm, one black nail, four penetrating genitals, seventeen penetrative genitals, no ass, almost no shoulders, one short neck, one head, two golden eyes, a flat nose with two nostrils, one mouth, around eighty teeth, five tongues, two ear holes, no external earflaps, twenty-six black horns . . .

Can you imagine it?

hOtBttm: Ah. . . . How specific.

Hunt1ng4love: Do I frighten you?

hOtBttm: Yes, a little.

Hunt1ng4love: Don't worry. I won't hurt you.

hOtBttm: Thanks, hahaha.

Of course, he thinks I'm kidding—stupid fuck.

hOtBttm: What are your hobbies?

Hunt1ng4love: Watching the sun set and sunbathing.

hOtBttm: Did the sun not set on your home planet?

Hunt1ng4love: It didn't. Nor was the night sky as splendid. Compared to the Earth, it was a dull place.

hOtBttm: So you like the Earth?

Hunt1ng4love: Nah. It is desolate. You?

hOtBttm: It's hard to say. I'm just living life, you know?

Hunt1ng4love: If I could leave here, yesterday is not soon enough.

hOtBttm: Please take me with you.

Hunt1ng4love: Depending on how today goes . . .

There is a naked human standing in the mirror with the physique of a lump of cheese. It is a work of art that I have created by grinding up my own body, but, truly, this "man's" flesh makes my mouth water. A beautiful body is more than worth its weight in gold. Like a cake, it is worth slicing into eight and wolfing it down as foamy blood builds up at the corners of your mouth with every greedy swallow. But since I can't eat myself, I must eat others. The people I will eat are standing in a never-ending line.

By now, dear reader, you must have input my life patterns into your mind. Since I have completed changing my form, I've now got to practice its appropriate movements and get dressed. You'll pretty much be able to predict my actions. Whether you like it or not, you are thinking about me. It's not taken long for you to get used to me. Might I say, dear reader, that I have permeated your life? Have I succeeded? Have I failed? You won't be able to get me out of your head for four days at the very least. You might even be looking out for me when you take the subway, keeping your eyes peeled for someone swaying under the weight of their obnoxiously large backpack. You might even see me moaning as I climb the stairs. You might even scream as I run out of the wrong bathroom. The chances of it are incredibly slim, but you might even swipe right on me, make a date, and drip with sweat as you ardently mouth my genitals or thrust your genitals into whichever of my holes takes your fancy. Soaked in your ecstasy, you may be gobbled up, or you might become my twelfth partner. But you'll never know,

not even if you were to rise from the dead.

Who am I, where did I come from and why, what am I doing with my life, what was I thinking before sex, what was I thinking during sex, and what was I thinking when I depart after sex—these are questions, dear reader, that you will never be able to answer. You will never come face-to-face with me as long as you live. You'd never know it even if you did, so it's the same as if you never will. I won't bear a grudge if you feign ignorance, dear reader. Ignore me as much as you please. Forget me. Forgetting is the best course of action. Aren't you curious as to why I am suddenly waxing lyrical? It's because our story is almost over. Although I don't know when it'll end. It's just a feeling. Goodbyes are normally saved for the moment of parting, but since the date and time of our departure is unknowable, I wish to say mine in advance. Farewell, dear reader. I will continue my adieus until we part. I will infinitely enlighten you to the finitude of my being.

The elevator sends me underground. As I wait for the train, I see myself reflected in the glass of the safety doors and do my best to pull myself together. The train duly arrives and opens its sides. Abominable passengers have filled all the seats with their asses that are stuffed full of shit and farts, crammed tightly together, leaving no gaps and no intention of giving up a spot for the likes of me. . . . It would be great if everyone, except for me, became unhappy. Please put a little more effort into becoming unhappy. I don't know how to make myself happy. Come and try crying to me about the measly cockups you call your lives. I'll wipe your tears and console you, all the while taking comfort in the knowledge that there's someone out there who's got it worse than me. It won't be easy, but I'll try to cry with you. Give me a chance to pity someone. It's utterly unfair for me to be the only one that has to hear the clicking of tongues. Tutting is no comfort to me! JUST DIE! Go ahead and destroy the Earth, you fucking bastards! Why me?! I've lost control. How tedious. I'm sick of pretending that everything is all right. . . .

I've calmed down now. Spitting out how I truly feel has cleared my head. Dear reader, are you still there? I've come back. I'm sitting sweetly in the corner of a train heading to my destination. I won't shout. I won't swear. I won't blame anyone else. I won't apologize when I'm not sorry. I'll get a little shut eye before I meet him. My . . . apologies, goodbye.

The clouds are growing dark and heavy. The cold wind blows sharp and furious. Soon it will rain. I'm sitting, waiting for him, on a wooden bench gone flaccid from sucking up the humidity. We've made plans to meet in the park before walking to a motel. Ah, raindrops are starting to wet the ground. But not enough to warrant an umbrella, yet. Since I wore a waterproof tracksuit—matching quite well with my hiking bag!—a few drops of rain won't hurt me. When will he show up? It's been ten minutes already. I'm someone who values time as much as life. Although, I don't really have any intention of valuing his life.

—I'm here. Could you step out a bit more?

—Huh? I don't see you. I'm sitting on the bench over here.
Hurry up. Why weren't you on time?

—Ah, sorry. Please walk fifty meters over here. Pretty please.
You're going to have to walk this way anyways when we go to
the motel.

My heart tries to bully me into taking out my blades,
but I neatly tuck it away beneath my ribs and, thinking I
have nothing to lose, follow his orders. However, all I can
see are the dreary lawns, skinny saplings tied to support
stakes, and rain-drenched pigeons.

—Where are you?

—Three more steps.

—Geez, hurry up!!

—Yeah, yeah, that's it.

BAM.

A steel pipe crashes into the back of my head. Helpless,
I collapse, slamming my chin into the brick path. A viscous
milklike liquid gushes from the rip in my scalp. It pushes
its way through my hair, cuts across my cheek, and clings
to my lips and the tip of my nose before drip, drip, dripping to the ground. It's been a long time since I've tasted

my own blood. Tart and bittersweet. My arms and legs are stuck at two apiece. I may be dazed, but it feels that way. It seems my body has not returned to its pretransformed form. The blow wasn't strong enough to snap my rubber bands, but I'm not stable. I'm growing weaker by the second, like a balloon flying through the sky, vomiting out its air. Right on cue, I hear the sounds of an excited gang surrounding me. *Did you knock him out? No, he's just pretending.* I've really ballsed it up this time. A tremendous cock-up. I'm fucking screwed. It's not that I've lost the thread, but rather it is about to snap. . . .

They are stomping on the masterpiece I slaved over as if they were mincing meat. I am loath to show them the real me. If I'm going to be stomped, I'll be stomped as a human, and if I'm going to die, I'll die as a human. Can you understand the agony of hating humans so much but shoving that hatred aside to look just like one? The desire to become a member of society always overpowers the shame of being embraced by their system. There's nothing worse than having my hideousness incur ridicule or cause some to be struck with fear. I will use every last bit of strength to hold on to my mimicry of humanity.

Pow powpow pow-bambambambam pow bam powpowpow pow bam pow bambambambam. I'm heating up like corn kernels in a microwave, but I'm holding tight to keep bits of me from flying off with all the strength I've used to suck tits and all the strength I've used to suck cock. So thankfully, when my leg breaks, a human leg breaks. And when my ribs snap and my skull cracks, it looks like a human's body parts. Unfortunately, I can't do anything to stem the flow of my white blood. It's like magma, unable to stand the pressure and forcing through cracks in the rocks. Splash! Splatter! As soon as the gloopy blood sprays over their faces and chests, these fucking bastards get scared and one by one stop what they're doing. *Woah, woah, what the fuck? H-he really is an alien!?* I can't hold back and laugh, HAHAHAHAHAHAHAHAHAHA. The jostling of my ribs might make me pass out, but there are no signs of the laughter stopping. My blood is not just *blood*, dear reader, it's acid blood that can dissolve human flesh, HAHAHA! They all back away. Their eyes will surely be shooting out blood from the pain of their skin melting off. I'm in no state to even twitch, but if I were, I would separate their bottom jaws from their upper jaws, making it impossible for them to cause a ruckus with their screaming—what a shame. It's more than enough to hear my own screaming. I have no space in my mind for the screams of others. As the little fuckers scatter, I am enveloped in silence. Piss off home, you bastards. Go run to your parents, brothers, or sisters and beg them to wipe the shit from your ass. And if you have no family, do it yourself, HAHAHAHAHAHA!

Farewell. I am dying, dear reader. Albeit, just a little faster than before. More like my death has been moved up on the schedule. There's no comparing my self-healing capabilities with a human's—I'm saying, my ability to recover is no joke! All I need is a few days' good rest, and I'll be able to return to my previous peaceful pace.

Thunder roars and lightning strikes. A sudden downpour. The net that had bound my whole body finally releases its hold. All the fish flood out in a whooooosh. This was not my intention. The stinging cold rain is sapping what little energy remains in me. Ah, I have changed into something like the viscera of a chicken or pig, washed in the pouring rain. The wounded human is a wounded alien life-form. The wounds didn't go anywhere, they came to me as they were. Surely no one would mess around with a severely injured alien? Since you never know if there may be a bacterial transfer, or if it may suddenly rise up and strike out.

But am I indeed alive? Am I a living, breathing organism? It doesn't feel real. Unending thoughts are already streaming over the threshold of life. I wish the rain would stop. At the moment, I can't take a single step. The most

I am capable of is i n f l a t i n g and deflating in the wind like a trash bag. G o o n a h e a d o f m e. I'll m a k e m y w a y to the subway soon enough.

Half a day later, I arrive at the subway station. If I pull my body together, it responds to my commands thirty seconds later and f o l l o w s. A splashing s o u n d e c h o e s t h r o u g h o u t the platform. The rainwater has not dried from the hollows and c r e v i c e s o f m y r a g g e d b o d y. This station is as empty as a newly e x c a v a t e d cave. The cave c o n t i n u e s t o w i d e n. I sit—no, lie in a chair and w a i t a n e t e r n i t y for the train. Forty pairs of train doors s p r i n g o p e n, but there w a s n o n e a m o n g t h e m that I could enter. Not because there were t o o m a n y p a s s e n g e r s —who knows where they all could have disappeared to; I didn't see a s i n g l e o n e —but because I was stuck in a s t a t e o f s u s p e n d e d a n i m a t i o n, incapable of hearing a train a r r i v e, g e t t i n g u p, and s t e p p i n g t h r o u g h t h e d o o r s at the right time. It was almost as if t h e y s e t i t u p f o r t h e d o o r s t o c l o s e before I could get on board. I couldn't even make it onto the train when I was lying on the ground right in front of the doors. A s s o o n a s t h e d o o r s o p e n , t h e y s t i r u p a w i n d s o f i e r c e and immediately close again. Or did the train just depart without opening the doors at all? They might not have even been stopping. It's possible the train has not yet come. Ah, I can't trust my own powers of perception. I am utterly trapped in this place, with not even a mouse. Behind me are the stairs; in front of me are the doors. The steps are growing taller; the doors are growing fewer. I can only hope that it's the delirium.

And then, I am sprawled out on the train, snoring. The lights flicker on, then off, repeatedly. The hanging handles fall in unison to one side, then return to their proper positions. When the train departs, I roll to the back, then roll forward when it stops. How strange a two-footed person has yet to show up. I can't even spot anyone with one foot, or no feet at all. What could the suffocating crowds be doing if they aren't clogging up the trains? Did they jump in front of a train? Get mangled in the wheels? Am I dreaming? If this keeps up, I'm scared I won't ever wake up from this dream. The train rat-ta-ta rattles as it speeds along. The lights flicker off and on and off and on, the hanging handles s w i n g   i n   s y n c   t o   o n e   s i d e, then back in place. W h e n   t h e   t r a i n   d e p a r t s I   r o l l   t o   t h e   b a c k,   a n d,   a r r ??   a t   t h e ?tion, I   r o l l   t o   t h e   f r?nt. Till death do   I   r e p e a t ???   R o l l o l o l o l o l i n g ?   I   d i d w r o n g ??   P l e a s e   f o r g i v e   m e ?   I t ' s   a l l   m y f a u l t ???   P l e a s e   l e t   m e   o u t   o f   h e r e ??? P l e a s e   s e n d   m e   h o m e ???   T u c k   m e i n t o   b e d ???   P l e a s e ?   W h a t e v e r   I d i d   w r o n g ?   L e t   m e   b e g   y o u r   f o r - g i v e n e s s ? ? ? ? ?   I   d i d   w r o n g ???? I t ' s   m y   f a u l t ?   I   d i d   w r o n g ???

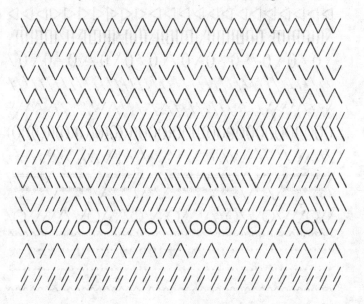

/// /// /// /// /// /// /// /// /// /// ///
O O O O O O O O O O O O O
/···/···/···/···/···/···/···/···/···/···/···/···/
\O\O\O\O\O\O\O\O\O\O\O\O\O\
‹‹‹
◁·O·O·O·O·O·O·O·O·O·O·O·O·O·O·O·O·O·▷
/O/O/O/O/O/O/O/O/O/O/O/O/O/
\\\
ⅩⅩⅩⅩⅩⅩⅩⅩⅩⅩⅩⅩⅩⅩ
ᐱOᐱOᐱOᐱOᐱOᐱOᐱOᐱOᐱOᐱOᐱOᐱOᐱO
VOVOVOVOVOVOVOVOVOVOVOVOV
▷▷▷▷▷▷▷▷▷▷▷▷▷▷◁◁◁◁◁◁◁◁▷▷▷
\[[[[O]]]]/O̅O̅O̅[O]]\[O]]O]]\[O]]/[[[O]]\O̅/[O̅O̅O̅]]\
\O/O\O/\O/O\O/\O/O\O/\O/\O/O\O/
///
V/\/\\\\V/\/\////////\/\\V/\/\V////\/\\\\
OOO))OOOOOOOOO)))OO(OOO(((((O(O(O)(O)((O))))O)
//\\V//\V//\/\\\V//\/\V///\/\/\V//\
****◇**◇*******◇*◇***◇***◇***\\
◇*****◇**◇*******◇**◇***◇***◇***◇
\\O\\VOV/O//\\\\O\VO/\\\OV/\\\\\O/
ᔕᔕᔕᔕᔕᔕᔕᔕᔕᔕᔕᔕᔕᔕᔕᔕᔕᔕᔕᔕᔕᔕᔕᔕᔕᔕᔕᔕᔕᔕ
....
....
ᔕᔕᔕᔕᔕᔕᔕᔕᔕᔕᔕᔕᔕᔕᔕᔕᔕᔕᔕᔕᔕᔕᔕᔕᔕᔕᔕᔕᔕᔕ
OOOOOOOOOOOOOOOOOOOOOOOOOOO

* * *

Hello there. Although you may not care to know, I have been holed up at home for a week, wrapped deep in blankets, not moving a muscle. My blankets have become thick and sticky like a slice of bread slathered in jam. Sprawled out in bed, pouring with sweat, dripping with drool, and leaking blood, I shat myself. The bright white blankets are indelibly stained with me. The stench is h o r - r e n d o u s. Have you been well, d e a r r e a d e r ? I am currently s h e d d i n g m y s k i n. My form peeks out hazily from beneath the s e m i t r a n s p a r e n t g e l a t i n o u s s l o u g h. With every breath, my molted skin crinkles and tightens. I slowly sit up, removing the blankets. F r a g m e n t s of my dead skin t u m b l e down. G r o a n i n g, I sluggishly s t r e t c h, and the skin at my side goes P O P ! and bursts open. My three feet press down on the floor, and I stand up, t r u d g e o v e r t o the wall, and o p e n a w i n d o w. In a flash, a beam of l i g h t c u t s t h r o u g h and g i v e s m e t h e e n e r g y I n e e d. My skin dries to a crisp like the flaky outer layers of an onion. I s h a k e m y s e l f l i k e a d o g, a m a s s i n g a pile of skin flakes on the floor. I w a n t n o t h i n g m o r e than to run straight to the mirror and see my newborn body r e f l e c t e d b a c k at me, but I must first s a t i s f y m y h u n g e r.

Opening the refrigerator, I rip into any raw meat that comes into my hands. No, I just swallow it whole. It is so delicious that my eyes are about to flip in my skull. I pour whole chunks of food into the long-neglected, mossy fish tank. The stomach that has been floating aimlessly in the filthy water comes running, and gobbles down the meat. Digestive liquids bubble and gurgle. Blood pumps, and cells revive. Bones harden as bones should. In just one hour, I have cleared out a month's worth of provisions, but I haven't shed a single tear. I can always go out on the hunt again, since I'm never going to leave this planet anyway. My body, which had been reduced to half its size, has regained its full weight. As the life slowly returns to my body, I push it to the bathroom and fill the tub with hot water. I will soak what's left of my molted skin and slough it off. And catch up on masturbating, sloshing the water. After sudsing up in the bath and drying off, I sit in the pilot seat and pull up the screen to check tens, if not hundreds, of messages. They'll be jam-packed with people cursing me. I'm sorry, I couldn't make it to our date. I couldn't satisfy you. But because I failed to keep my promises, haven't you escaped death? Or

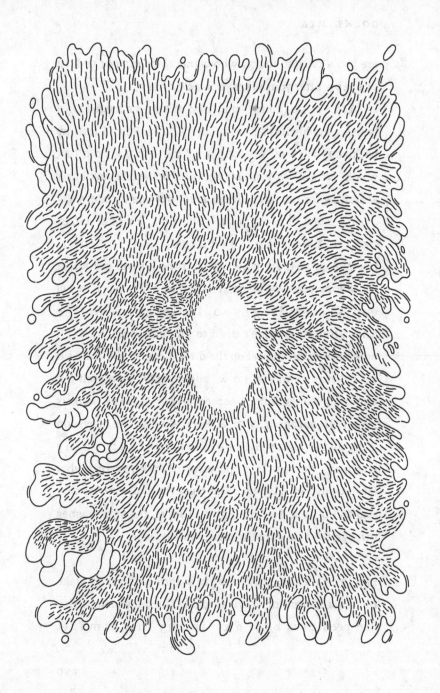

are you a twisted fucker who wants to be murdered in ecstasy after your climax has come?

After setting up my new schedule, I launder my blankets, sheets, and pillows. Since I lost my backpack, I can't organize my tools, wah wah wah. My shiny babies will be anxiously searching for me. I call their names out one by one: saw one, saw two, saw three, knife one, knife two, knife three, knife four, hammer one, hammer two. I will not forget these four years we've spent together. I'll buy new tools just like you. I've got enough clothes and shoes, so I don't need to buy any more. I POP! outside my ship and set up the drying racks in a sunny meadow and quickly tire myself out as I hang the laundry. I cocoon myself in fresh blankets and fall, yet again, into a deep sleep. The television is on, and as always, I dream of the exploding planet. I escape in a spaceship, not knowing what fate awaits my relations, and then the hull catches fire, and as I plead for my life, the ship crashes through the rain onto the muddy forest floor.

My screams follow me into reality and wake me up at eleven forty-five at night. The television, which had been blocked out in my nightmare, is still tickling me with its murmuring sound and radiating glow. Passively, I watch the humans squirming on the screen as I wriggle in my blankets when, all of a sudden, I am hungry. My body whines, telling me that it doesn't want frozen food, but fresh-caught meat. I support its demands wholeheartedly. Since I no longer have my trusted tools at hand to break down flesh and pack it up to take home, I'll have to eat up every bit of my kill from head to toe. My body is brimming with confidence. *What I ate in the morning has already become pellets of shit.* To be honest, I am a teensy bit frightened since this is the first time I've molded my body into shape after the attack. But has there ever been a time when I defeated my body? I am beholden to my body's every demand. Dear reader, this is how I live.

pOw3r★tOp: Wanna meet up rn? I'm close.

A slim thirty-one-year-old man is plucked from the spaceship. He must be taken to the public toilets at the head of the trail by twelve thirty. We lope along the path sparsely lined with streetlamps. He flaps his way down the path like a ravenous baby bird. There's something off in the symmetry of his body, causing him to appear somewhat discombobulated. It seems that either one leg is shorter than the other, or perhaps one of his shoulders or hips is askew. I'll make a belated confession. I wasn't able to complete my physical reconstruction. A poor job from start to finish. I didn't put my heart into capturing his bilateral symmetry. I wound up making a bedraggled starfish. Please keep in mind that barely a day has passed since I shed my skin. I've done my best. It's not like I fucked up the top and bottom halves! I'm praying that I'll be able to manage holding myself in this state for the next couple of hours. And it just so happens to be my first time going out at night. The fact that I'm going through all of this trouble just to have sex in a filthy bathroom shows I'm not of sound mind or body. A public toilet is not the most appropriate location for my work. Since there are so many people going in and out, you're stuck choking down your voices and sweating in a tiny cubicle. It's such a headache when you're breaking down meat and cleaning up afterward. Humans who get off on the thrill of messing around in a bathroom are number one on my "to avoid" list. But it's a different story when it's past midnight at a public toilet in the middle of a forest.

Passing the sign marking the trail, I climb up the stone steps. The dark bathroom is like an abandoned house. As soon as I flip the switch, the fluorescent bulbs light up its innards. The tile floors are decorated with patches of slime and piss stains with accents of mud and gravel scattered here and there. Even the sinks and drains are blanketed in the corpses of mosquitoes and mayflies. . . . I don't know why I've come here. What reason could I possibly have for endangering the location of my spaceship and dragging out my miserable body? When my core rule is:

※ Hookup locations must be at a distance of 3 km or more. (That is, locations must not be within walking distance.)

Why am I completely ignoring it? I chew over my reckless actions and hit myself in the head as I wait for p0w3r★t0p by the entrance to the toilets. Do you think this might be a sting operation set up by the police? Have they detected my identity—a sex-crazed alien—and reached out on purpose to arrest me? That would explain his extraordinary flirting technique. What made him pick this specific bathroom? If he's not staying at the lodge, there's no reason for him to pick somewhere so close to my house. Isn't that suspicious? It's clear that this man knows me. And if, in a million to one chance, he's one of my own kind . . .

I will ask him his (there'd be no point in using these pronouns) name and tell him mine. This is how our conversation would begin. It might not even end by morning. We'll go over every minutiae, asking, *Where is your spaceship, are you sleeping well, what do you dream about, what are you eating to survive, how are you managing your sex drive, do you have any friends or lovers, how much do you miss your family, what do you think of when you think of home, what are the shortcomings and drawbacks of this place, . . . and why have we not been able to make contact for all this time?* We will never again be separated. Even if we had never seen each other's face back home, in a matter of minutes we'll become each other's one friend and only family. We may even start a family of our own. Thirty kids will be enough. The spaceship will be full of chatter. Even if I wake up from a nightmare, I won't be alone alone alone. There will be someone beside me who will listen to my recurring nightmares. I am happy.

Over time we grow bolder and head out as a group to hunt without any fancy tricks. Paying no mind to the food as they scream or throw up blood in the streets in broad daylight, we are delirious with satisfaction and gustatory joy. Our children will mate with each other and breed veteran hunters. Humans will have to be careful outdoors. They'll have to quake with fear at the thought of going out. Is a house safe because you call it home? In a fit of anger, we will try to stamp out the human seed, but then stop ourselves and raise them as livestock, as pets. We will occupy the earth. This is our new home!

—You got here quick.

A large, hairy man (196 cm, 110 kg) appears and climbs up the steps five at a time. The sweet scent of his body lotion stabs a headache into my temples. He's wearing a checked shirt and dark-wash jeans with a leather belt. The hair on his head is thinning. On top of being fifteen minutes late, he's being snarky with me, and that makes me want to knock him down a peg. As he tells me to hurry up and get inside, he grabs me by my wrist and drags me into the bathroom. His fingers are thick, sticky, and reeking of cigarettes. I'll have to be careful not to swallow them on accident. His overbearing attitude turns me off, but I follow him anyway. That's right, hurry up and use me . . . I won't forget to make you pay for it.

With a placid face, he gestures toward the sink. *Bend over. Pull down your pants.* The dead bugs crunch and stick to my palms. He slaps my ass hard. Until it turns bright red. He spreads my cheeks, spits in the hole, and unzips his pants. *This is gonna hurt. Hold tight. Yeah? Got it?* He thrusts his hard cock straight into my asshole. It doesn't hurt. I see my unfocused eyes, my shaking body in the mirror that seems clouded by frost. My genitals are slapping against the edge of the sink counter. He fists my hair, wrangling me as if he's trying to break a horse while grunting, *Ah ah, fuck, haaaaaa, fuck.* The worry that my transformation may come undone is far greater than any feeling of stimulation his baubles are giving my anus.

He signals that he wants to change positions. I strip off my top and lie bare-backed on the counter. Frighteningly fast, he spreads my legs, rubbing my body on the slippery insect corpses. I must be ripping off their legs and wings. Why did I come to meet him? To become his tool? I need to feel myself, as a warm body, being used by anyone. A smile sneaks across my lips. It's ludicrous how much I depend on the pleasure I derive from these worthless humans penetrating my fake asshole. He's not one of my kind. He's not a police officer trying to arrest me either. He's just a human. *Ah ah ah ah ah, fucking take it, ah ah ah!* His semen floods my hole. I am overcome with a sharp pain of an orgasm. Is this joy or is it sorrow? He removes his dick from me and

transforms. His colossal mouth, layered like an onion, creaks as it rotates open. He bites down on the sink. I narrowly escape, tumbling to the floor. There's no time to be shocked, so I transform as well. *Well, would you look at that?* His tens of eyes slowly blink vertically and in unison fix on me. He is over three times my size, and nimble as well. He threatens my life as his nine arms and legs flail. His axe-like toenail, sawlike fingernail. There is nowhere to run but toward the toilets. There is no reply to my questions of *Who are you?* and *Where did you come from?* as he casts his tentacles in a wide net, cutting off any escape routes. His expert attack slices off my horn and rips my leathery skin, causing blood to trickle out. On the other hand, I'm unable to make a single mark; I'm out of my depth. He is toying with me, batting me about like a ball with the florid motion of his limbs. It'd be no fun if he killed me right away. Public toilets reeking of blood. Not of his blood, only mine. I am tossed to the ceiling, pierced and stabbed as I crash to the floor, and I am thrown again. I can't focus. Then I think of home—of the meat left in my refrigerator, and of insatiable desire —and try to find a moment when I land on three feet. Ready your legs. Jump with all your might. Throw your body toward the little window. Hide in the forest rolling among the fragments of glass and cement. N O W R U N ! ! ! I stumble through the trees, getting farther and f a r t h e r away from my spaceship as I run in the opposite direction the demented monster flies at me s h o o t i n g l i q u i d f r o m i t s t a i l My face is black in fear I keep looking behind me A b r a n c h s t a b s m y e y e Scrape the bottoms of my feet T r i p o n r o c k s a n d f a l l o v e r Again and again I pick myself up and keep r u n n i n g r u n n i n g r u n n i n g Out of breath and dizzy His relentless shadow is glued to me H i s a r m s a n d l e g s s t r e t c h o u t l i k e w i n g s The moonlight is so beautiful Save me Save me S a v e m e S a v e m e I've lost the fight I surrender I've failed I am a failure I'm dying I ' m d y i n g a l o n e I must tell you my name

it is

Muhi libilip liplip

they call me

Mumu

for short

cute
isn't
it
I
am
in
your
care

0 km

A NOTE FROM THE TRANSLATOR ------

Upon first reading the self-published iteration of *Walking Practice*, I was immediately drawn to the charismatic voice Dolki Min created for the first-person narrator, Mumu, and was bodily affected by the writing; I laughed out loud in a doctor's waiting room when Mumu teased the readers; I felt my guts wrench while riding the bus as Mumu made the novel's first gory kill; I felt the weight of every pained movement Mumu made to escape assailants push me farther and farther down into my bed. The nakedness of Mumu's direct connection to the reader ensnared me and I felt compelled to translate the voice I was feeling in my mind, that I felt I knew so well, and so intimately after our initial encounter.

The physicality of the text and the way it embodies and weaponizes conventional understandings of sex and gender as a way to feed the violent hunger of Mumu's loneliness is what makes *Walking Practice* a profoundly queer work of literature. Faced with literal alienation from human society and the struggle to survive in an inhospitable world, Mumu wrestles with their decision to use humans for pleasure and sustenance and their desire for acceptance, companionship, and love. The language of *Walking Practice* is sensual, in both sensory and seductive meanings, and contains a lot of textured verbs and onomatopoeia, which are difficult to convey in English. This challenged me as a translator to make choices that evoked a similar bodiliness and plunder the depths of my vocabulary for any and all genital-derived terms and phrases in order to dismember genitals from gender and walk the organ-strewn line between ravenous lover and serial killer.

Physicality is not only expressed in the language the novel uses, but also in how it visualizes the mental state of the narrator through the disruption of legibility. In the source text, this is expressed more orthographically due to the fact that, in Korean, the parts of a sentence are marked by postpositions, which make the meaning more trackable when words are torn apart and stitched together. The limitations of how English is written and read created further challenges when trying to express this facet of the Korean text in the most legible, yet still visually striking and disruptive, manner. Ultimately, the solution resided in moving away from replicating the Korean technique and into a more technical adjustment to how the words are presented on the page. While at first it may look like a typesetting error, the expansion and contraction of the English text is the strategy I devised as a way to visualize in English the way the Korean text separates and clusters characters when the tension breaks and Mumu's consciousness reverts to something less human and indecipherable to others.

Translating this novel at a time when queer activists in Korea are fighting for an anti-discrimination bill and when the rights of queer Americans are under sustained attack reinforces my goal as a translator to make queer narratives visible and visceral. While the novel may be positioned under the umbrella of speculative fiction, many of Mumu's fears and the dangers they face are mirrored in the fears and dangers faced by queer people, not only in Korea, but around the world: the fear of being out-ed, the threat of persecution, the potential to be met with violence in the pursuit of love. *Walking Practice* is a novel that yearns for community as much as it is a novel that plays with notions of gender and sexual expression.

To honor both the queer and translation communities that have supported me and this project over the years, I'd like to thank my friend and fellow translator, Soje, for thinking of me when they read the initial self-published form of *Walking Practice* and gifting me their copy, and to thank my advisors and mentors at the University of East

A NOTE FROM THE TRANSLATOR

Anglia, Cessi Rossi and B. J. Epstein, for their guidance
when I was working on the sample translation as part of
my MA project, and to thank my fellow Smoking Tigers
for encouraging the more experimental style choices. And
thanks most of all to Dolki Min for entrusting me with this
precious book.

— VICTORIA CAUDLE